2/18/23 To Nina,
I still miss
your
smile and
friendship -
Love
B

THE OLD CART WRANGLER, THE NEW SILENCE, AND OTHER NOTIONS:

Monologues and Short Fiction

BRIAN PRICE

THE OLD CART WRANGLER, THE NEW SILENCE, AND OTHER NOTIONS: MONOLOGUES AND SHORT FICTION.

ISBN: 978-1-71679-291-5

Library of Congress Control Number: 2020913580

Portions of this book are works of fiction. Any references to historical events, real people, or real places are used fictitiously. Other names, characters, places, and events are products of the author's imagination, and any resemblances to actual events or places or persons, living or dead, are entirely coincidental. Portions of this book are works of nonfiction. Certain names and identifying characteristics have been changed.

Editing by Eleanor Price.
Design and illustration by Evie Brosius.

Published by Brian Price. Indianapolis, IN.

Printed in the United States of America.

Performance and Publishing Credits

The Collapse of the Twentieth Century Was So Gradual*
March 28, 1997, Mark Time Radio Show, Minicon 32, Minneapolis, Minnesota
David Ossman – voice; David Emerson – piano

Clones Day Parade*
July 6, 2001, Mark Time Radio Show, CONvergence, Minneapolis, Minnesota
David Ossman – voice; Mike Wheaton – piano

Closed Mouths and Narrow Necks*
May 29, 2002, The Yellow House, National Audio Theatre Festivals, West Plains, Missouri
David Ossman – voice; Thom Hoglen – bass; Eric Elder – saxophone

Your Mileage May Vary*
July 5, 2002, Mark Time Radio Show, CONvergence, Minneapolis, Minnesota
Richard Fish – voice; Eleanor Price – flute (added in August 2017)

A Cure for Science*
July 2, 2004, Mark Time Radio Show, CONvergence, Minneapolis, Minnesota
David Ossman – voice; Jim ten Bensel – trombone

The Old Cart Wrangler's Saga: Cart 437 or The Long Way Around*^
July 7, 2006, Mark Time Radio Show, CONvergence, Minneapolis, Minnesota
David Ossman – voice

The Tiniest Souls*
July 6, 2007, Mark Time Radio Show, CONvergence, Minneapolis, Minnesota
David Ossman – voice

Under the Broken Tree Bridge*
July 3, 2008, Mark Time Radio Show, CONvergence, Minneapolis, Minnesota
Eleanor Price – voice; Keith Spears – piano

The Secrets of Blackberry Pie
October 2014, San Francisco Public Library, San Francisco, California
Bruce Allen – voice

The Old Cart Wrangler's Saga: Cart 437 2.0: The Continuing Story of a Man and His Shopping Cart*^
June 9, 2016, Hear Now Festival, Kansas City, Missouri
David Ossman – voice

Verifying Graffiti
June 6, 2018, The Brick, Kansas City, Missouri
Richard Fish – voice

The Old Cart Wrangler's Saga: The Entire Tale, including Cart 437 3.01: Potemkin^
June 6, 2018, The Brick, Kansas City, Missouri
David Ossman – voice; Rev. Dwight Frizzell – woodwinds;
Julia Thro – guitar; Patrick Alonzo Smith Conway – percussion;
Tony Brewer – sound effects

Portions of The New Silence poems can be heard in:

Silence Is Coming – a podcast by Marjorie Van Halteren and Brian Price
Released January 8, 2019 on electroacousticalpoeticalsociety.com, Lille, France
Marjorie Van Halteren – voice; Brian Price – voice

The New Silence
Written and directed by Brian Price
June 8, 2019, The Hear Now Festival, Kansas City, Missouri
Dion Graham – voice; Jane Oppenheimer – voice;
Jason Kao Hwang – violin, effects

---

* Live recordings of these pieces available on Loose Wheels and Narrow Necks: Cart 437 and Other Slightly Dystopian Tales, by Brian Price, performed by David Ossman.
Please visit: www.downpour.com/loose-wheels-and-narrow-necks?sp=208664

^ Live recordings of these pieces available on The Old Cart Wrangler's Saga: A Full Blown, Full Length, Fully Baked Comic Monologue by Brian Price, performed by David Ossman.
Please visit: www.downpour.com/the-old-cart-wrangler-s-saga?sp=278221

The Entire Great Northern Audio Theatre catalogue is available on:
www.downpour.com/catalogsearch/result/?q=Brian+Price

For a complete history of the Mark Time Radio Show and a complete listing of all Great Northern Audio Theatre productions and news please visit:
www.greatnorthernaudio.com/

The Tiniest Souls first appeared in DOORWAYS MAGAZINE #5, 2008.

Cart 437 first appeared in the Vermillion Literary Project 2007, University of South Dakota, 2007.

The Hill first appeared in the online magazine, COMBAT.ws, July 2005.

For Bill Strobridge—
The first kid I ever met who wanted to be a writer and said it out loud.

Thinking about it, I grew up in Arlington, Virginia, in a neighborhood that was torn down for a highway. Many of my childhood memories are buried there somewhere under eight lanes of tar.
Maybe I do take all this stuff personally.

- Brian Price

Contents

Foreword

Notion is a funny little word. It can be a thought or a concept or a conceit, or it can be the bits and bobs you find in a sewing kit, the thread scraps and pins and broken buttons. Notions make things.

For as long as I can remember, my father has had a special acquaintance with the way words sound versus what they mean. Thus *notion,* thus *new silence*. They're things that sound a little funny, a little mixed up. But they sound good too, and powerful when you say them out loud. There's an audible lilt to some of these tales.

Perhaps he would say it came from his mother, but my father has always had a way of rearranging words, reorganizing them, maybe recategorizing them to become something else entirely, an absurdist dream of what they were before. The echo of mundane is transmuted into a strange liminal space in these stories and poems, and a larger world of urban ephemera and pastoral complications lurks behind each page. I assure you that these spun words contain vastnesses, the way that when you look into a marble you can see a globe.

My father also teaches good habits: for example, keep a piece of paper and a pen on you at all times, just in case you come up with a good phrase. In case you stumble upon a world.

Invite these worlds over for the afternoon, get to know them. Worlds like words are meant to be said aloud, so twirl them about in your mouth and get to know their multiplanar surfaces. In short, enjoy.

- Eleanor Price

Introduction

Back five, six years ago, around the time of the last Mark Time Radio Show (*Cyber Bob and the Digital Nymph*), David Ossman and I were taking a little break and *Cart 437* came up. We'd always liked that piece. I liked it because *Cart 437* brings up the hard truth and not so far-fetched likelihood of working for Walmart at the tender age of 75. And for David—he just climbed into the character. He and the Wrangler are one and the same.

"You know, I perform *Cart 437* every now and then with my solo shows," David said. "But, you need to write another act or two. It's not finished yet."

That little comment brought up two things I didn't know. First, my monologues were starting to get out and find an audience on their own. That was pretty neat. And second, the monologues weren't through with me yet. They never are. I needed to keep writing. By 2018 the Old Cart Wrangler trilogy was complete, and the full-length show has been performed in Kansas City, outside Seattle, and hopefully someday in Hawaii.

Writing has always been a conversation for me. It's talking. It's finding the voice that finds the character that establishes the situation that creates a problem that has to be solved. For me the voice is always where it begins, the point of departure, because to write it down I have to hear it first, reading it aloud back and forth, back and forth. If I don't hear it, it doesn't seem real. And no matter how bizarre or silly the situation, for me it has to sound real. The character, the voice, the writer—we have to take this stuff seriously.

Same for the performer (and these pieces are meant to be performed).

The actor has to believe all this stuff. It has to soak in and then the character and voice have to pour out. The actor has to see and hear and feel that weirdness, that particular place. What's amazing is that they always do. That's what I love about theater—they make you believe in the craziest of worlds.

And there is a world in here, in this book, a connected world, a personal mythology. From the parking lot to the blackberry pie to the silence and even to the end of the bike trail. It's all connected. I'd ask the Cart Wrangler to draw you a map, but he'd say you don't need a map. Just follow the curbs and you'll get there.

I've always liked sound for sound's sake. It's such a leap of faith, the hope and glee of understanding something, anything, through the garbled translation of everyday human speech—one person saying something to the other and then both of them getting it. I don't get that. It's amazing. I don't know how we get anything through all those words. It's a miracle. And the words and sounds are made so much more interesting by these simple acts:

- Silliness—my mother saying Bumfrey Gocart for Humphrey Bogart.
- Rebellion—John Lennon's "A Spaniard In the Works."
- Entertainment—"The Button-Down Mind of Bob Newhart."
- Howling madness—Lord Buckley and Professor Irwin Corey.
- Absurdity—the prose poetry of Russell Edson.

I like hybrids, mishmashes, mixing styles and forms, trying to outrun the labels. But labels are part of language, right? Labels are how we locate and define things. Still, we may as well look for the edges. When is a poem not a poem but a play? When is a song not a song but a novel? When is an essay a fantasy? When is a monologue not a monologue?

Whoops, wait a minute—monologues are never monologues. They're dialogues. They're always dialogues. They're conversations. You're talking to somebody, right? An audience, yourself, the one person you were hoping was there.

Conversation is often collaboration. I've always liked collaboration, and I'm sure that collaboration is what has drawn me to theater, albeit audio theater, over all these years. The actors, musicians, producers, engineers, other writers—they all make their contributions and what sweet contributions they are. But maybe, because I'm lazy, impatient, cheap and unsure, I appreciate collaborations because there's always the hope that I'll get something for free. Somebody will come in and improve on the string of words I've made, and most of the time they do.

Finally, if there were a piece of advice I'd have to give, it would be this. I believe wanting to be a writer and wanting to be a cart wrangler are pretty much the same thing. All you have to do is get up every morning, grab hold, and push.

- Brian Price
December 2019

The Old Cart Wrangler, The New Silence, and Other Notions:

Monologues and Short Fiction

Brian Price

The Highway Is Like A River

1991

THE HIGHWAY IS LIKE A RIVER, and like a river it is never the same way twice. That's what she said to me and I should've believed her. She said if I went back through the hole in the fence the currents and the shadows would never be the same.

I've been up and down the emergency lanes on this stretch of road for I don't know how long. I should've believed her, but I can't. I just can't. The hole's gotta be along here somewhere. The traffic's thinned down some, so roll down your window and take a long look out at the side of the road. I know you can't see much from 60-70 miles per hour. The asphalt apron, the reflectors, the drainage ditches and the ragged bushes. They almost pulse going by—like light through a pinwheel. It all looks the same, but it's not. There are worlds back in there.

The interstate's loud. You don't realize it, but it roars and howls. Especially when you're down along its edge. When you're in it. When you're stopped. When your cell phone's dead. When there's trouble—a split radiator hose. A bald spare. When your dumb luck's run out. When you're leaning on your driver's side front quarter panel being buffeted and choked by semis.

It's so loud and the cars are going by sounding like they're saying—You Are. You Are. You Are. And you want to ask. I am what? What am I? You Are. You are. You are. That's all they say.

Now, here's what happened to me. I was driving home (maybe a little too fast) in my old Ford Escort hatchback with the bent steering column and stripped low gear and something blew and I careened 80 miles an hour across three lanes of traffic, horns blaring, tires screeching, almost got T-boned. Ground across the edge of the apron into a dull muddy stop in a dull muddy ravine.

I was out of the car, jumping around, full of adrenaline. All I could hear was you are, you are, you are. I was screaming and happy to be alive. That's when I saw her.

The Clover Leaf People aren't used to being seen. They can stand right on the side of the road and you'll never see them. You'll always be going by too fast. They can do about anything they want—wave, pull down their pants, throw rocks, and you won't see them, because you're not looking, nobody's looking, so they're just not there.

But I saw her and I could tell she realized—she'd been seen. She didn't expect that. She was coming towards the car like she assumed we were in different worlds. And then she stopped dead in her tracks. She looked at me and looked me in the eye and then looked down at herself like maybe she had something stuck to her. Like she was a target.

I said, I screamed because that's all you can do over traffic, "Can you help me? My phone's dead." And she came a little closer. I said, "I think I'm okay but my car's not and where's your car? And what're you doing out here?"

She said she lived there. And I said, "What, right here in the middle of the road?" And she said, "No," and she pointed, "You see that old board that crosses the ditch and then follows a path through the dead grass up the embankment over the rise to the fence?" I said, "Yeah." And she said, "That's where we live, through the hole in the fence."

She took my hand and led me. She said her name was Gnat. She talked a mile a minute. She was little and lithe and she made me ache. We ducked through the hole in the fence and the other side was like a kiss.

There's all these spaces in the world where you think nobody lives—

like the insides of interstate clover leaves, in culverts and down the middle of median strips. And that's where the Clover Leaf People live. They've got farms, well, not farms, but stuff growing. And kids. And plastic—but of course everybody's got plastic. They light fires and bed down in the backs of rusted, picked-over minivans.

I don't want you to think that the Clover Leaf People are like extras out of Peter Pan or from some sorta lost Mad Max movie. It's not that way. They just are. I don't know how they got there. Maybe they don't either. They live by being invisible in places where you assume nobody would be. Not a bad gig.

"But, where do you get your clothes?" I asked. "At the mall like everybody else," they said. It was a three-day trek across the Great Parking Lot to one of the Lesser Malls. Sometimes they overwintered in the lower levels of the south parking garage.

"And what do you eat?" I asked. "The highway is like a river and like a river it provides," they said.

We collected what fell and rolled and bounced off of trucks and finally came to rest along the edge of the interstate. We rooted through the wrecked and the stalled. We checked under the seats. Mostly we ate Twinkies and squirrel.

Gnat and I were about the same age. I was maybe eighteen and she said she was fifteen or seventeen or something. She pretty much ignored me for the first few months I was there. She'd saved me and then she ignored me. She said she expected me to disappear. But really it was the other way around, she expected herself to disappear. And it's like she finally just gave in. "I guess if you can see me, you must be mine," she said, because that's how she really thought.

"Do you think you'll always see me?" she asked with us in a van under a blanket, me curled around her. "I don't know," I said. "I don't even know why I can see you now."

"That's the problem," she said. "Maybe there'll be some day when you won't see me." We made love about a million times.

Sometimes I think maybe she had a kid. And I think maybe I see the kid at the mall. I wanna catch up and say, "Where's your mother? How's she doing? What'ch she say about me?" But, the kid just goes into the crowd and never comes out again.

"If you go, you may never find your way back," she said. "I know," I said, "Because the highway is like a river and like a river it can always change course."

We smiled. We didn't quite laugh. And we didn't make love the morning I left. All I wanted to do was go back for a couple of days, grab a couple of things, say goodbye. Just go back and say, "Don't worry. I'll be fine, Ma. I fell in love. I found this place."

"The highway is like a river and like in a river you can drown." But I didn't drown. I just walked along, stuck out my thumb and got a ride. I looked back and there was nothing there.

And there was nothing to say goodbye to either when I got back. Found Mortgage Heights, the old neighborhood where all the streets are named after vice presidents; but I couldn't find the cul-de-sac I grew up on. I couldn't find my family. I took a job doing something I didn't have to think about. Played third base on the company softball team.

Ever since, I've been searching. Cruising up and down this highway searching for the hole in the fence. It's the only home I'm going to find. The only one I want.

I don't know much, but I know this: There are really only three ways Americans get things accomplished in this world: by faith, luck, or sacrifice. I suppose there's hard work too, but that always seems a little extreme.

I'm most familiar with luck. It's a good system and I try to stick to it. It's the way I found Gnat. But luck's so fickle and so statistical. Aren't the odds always against us?

I've been thinking about what I've been doing wrong all this time. Maybe I've been going too slow when I should've been going too fast. Maybe what we need to do is do what I did before, when I saw her—

crash.

So, I've been thinking about making a sacrifice. I don't have anything, so maybe something of yours. Let's see if we can get this hunk of junk you're driving up to about 80, maybe 90 miles per hour and recreate the same conditions that happened the first time.

I can see you shaking your head, "no." That's okay. I can understand you not wanting to sacrifice yourself in a fiery crash for a total stranger, but what's the deal with your car? It's just a Buick. Okay, okay, how about this? We'll just pull off to the side and we'll get out and take in the scenery—the dull muddy ravine, the board, the path, the fence.

You are. You are. You are. The same declarations go by. I am. I am what. What am I? What do you think? Crazy? Delusional? Institutionalizeable?

I tell you what I know I am—close. This is really close. This is closer than I've been for a long time. She's close. Close like a whisper. I can feel it. And I can feel something I never knew I had—faith—the third of the three graces. Faith that I'd keep looking and she'd keep looking. Faith, like what is to be is to be. I hadn't thought about that. Home isn't just something one searches for. It must search for you, as well.

All this searching and it wasn't just dumb luck again. Luck is good for first times. Faith is for second chances.

There's Gnat—coming towards us out of the mist that's tangled in tall grass. The cars go by oblivious, because that's what they do. But, I can see her and I can see that she sees me.

I hope you don't mind if she takes a few things from your car. It's her way. It's the way of her people, the Clover Leaf People. My people now. My people again. People who came out of the cities and can no longer be seen. But that's okay—we only need to see ourselves.

I'm gonna leave you now. I'm going to catch up with Gnat. We'll find our own ratted out van and kiss and have kids.

The group will probably overwinter on the other side of the

interstate. We'll line up on the edge of the emergency lane like we're all ready to run a race, and we'll cross while the traffic eddies and swirls. We'll take good care, because the highway is like a river and like a river it is mighty and wide.

Closed Mouths and Narrow Necks

2002

I BELIEVE I'VE DISCOVERED WHY CIVILIZATION, as we know it, as it once was, as we hoped it would continue to be, is once again on the downhill trudge. I know you're anxious to know. But you must be patient. We all must be.

Here, hold this bottle. Take it. It's just a bottle of catsup. Just a simple condiment. Take the bottle and twist off the cap. Turn it upside down. Shake it. Shake it again. Spank it. Spank it more than twice. Spank it hard. Hold it high over your head. Jerk it. Threaten and curse the bottle. It'll do you no good and you already know why. You already know that you're participating in one of the most archetypical, ancient and fruitless struggles known to man.

So, hold the open end of the bottle up to your eye. Take a long look. There's plenty in there. You can see that. That's not the problem. You know the problem. Stick a forefinger far down the neck of the bottle. Pull. Wriggle. Twist. Coax. But nothing will come out. Including your finger.

You're feeling a little tense. A little sheepish. Pent up. Maybe penned in. That's all right. You're just feeling what's always been felt. What your forebearers always found. It's a scene that's been seen many times before. Oddly enough, your stomach rumbles.

You ask—what's this all got to do with civilization? And I'll say patience. All you've got to do is answer this simple question. What do the Picts, the Romans, the Ming Dynasty, and the Anasazi Indians of the great American Southwest all have in common? You'll ponder a moment and you'll say, "They're extinct," and you'll be right.

But, come on, what else? What else did these lost, noble, and proud civilizations have in common? You'll say, "Pottery," yeah, that's right—pottery. They all made pottery, and lovely pottery it was. And here's the kicker—what were the similarities in these museum-quality pieces? They all had narrow necks and useless spouts. As a matter of historical record, by the time each of one of these decrepit cultures collapsed and were chased under their aqueducts or out across the steppes, the spouts of their jars were so ornate and so damn narrow you couldn't squeeze a single drop out of them.

You got it now? All these civilizations starved to death. They turned their pots upside down and nothing came out. You see it in the Anasazi. They just stacked up their pots in the dusty corners of their cliff dwellings and were never heard from again. Meanwhile, the Mings got shanghaied by Genghis Khan while they were in the pantry trying to find something to eat that wasn't trapped in their precious over-glazed porcelains.

And the most horrific evidence of all lies perfectly preserved just across the Pentland Firth on the Isle of Hoy in an ancient and awful peat bog where archaeologists discovered the last known Pict—sword in hand, one leg in a puddle of tar, the other leg in the jaws of a saber-tooth tiger, and his free hand with a forefinger stuck inside the narrow neck of a Late Neo-Archaic work of earthenware. A work that looks, to this modern man, a lot like a modern-day catsup bottle.

And so the cycle continues. March on over to your local supermarket. The mouths of the bottles are getting smaller and smaller—be it olives or the various dressings, or the most dreaded of all condiments, Grey Poupon—you can't hope to coax anything out of those things.

So, I suppose this is goodbye. Like with so much knowledge, now that we know what we need to know, it does us no good. We can't shake hands with our forefingers trapped in these narrow necks. We can only quietly clink our catsup bottles and sit down in our chosen deserts and wait to be covered by the dying sands. Sand, of course, being the main ingredient of glass.

We can only have patience and wait. Like our distant ancestors half-buried on their savannas or ice flows, we can only hope and dream of a land where utility, for once, will overshadow design and there will be a grand era when a man can get his finger out of anything he puts it into.

The Old Cart Wrangler's Saga: Cart 437 or The Long Way Around

2006

WHEN I CAME TO THE MART I was 75 years old. At the time I hadn't expected to go back to work, but I'd owned some bad stock, drank a little more than I should… Betty died.

My neighbor, Fred, said, you oughta go to work at the Mart. "It ain't hard—get you out of the house." I went down there and I told them I didn't want any indoor job. I didn't want nothing to do with being no toothless greeter, smiling, putting stickers on things. I wanted to be outside. I didn't mind. I didn't care about the weather. I wanted to be a cart wrangler.

Management didn't think I'd be able to keep up. Heck, what was there to keep up with? I can push a shopping cart. I can push a row of shopping carts just as good as any kid. As a matter of fact, I taught those high school kids a few tricks. How to balance and ride a cart around a corner. How to make sure a bent basket don't get caught in the middle of a row. How to bend back a bent wheel. Do it my way, you'd have time for a smoke.

Out of the corner of my eye, even on the first day, I noticed there was one cart that wasn't nestled in with the rest. You'd chase it down, roll it on over and line it up; and the next thing you knew the cart'd be just a little ways sitting off next to the drinking fountain. Next time you looked, it'd be out in the parking lot squeezed between a mini-van and an SUV. Cart 437.

It didn't take me long to get a little bit of a reputation. I was the guy who'd go a ways out of his way to get the last cart. Most Mart employees wouldn't bother. They just wanted to go home and get their ears pierced or their butts tattooed, but if there was a cart out there I was going to go get it and bring it in.

I'd be the guy who'd push two or three wayward carts back across the dirt path of the vacant lot next to Kentucky Fried—their little wheels catching and dragging. I'd be the one to bother to check out by the dumpsters. I'd be the guy who'd hike out to the last light pole and make sure none were missing. More often than not I'd find Cart 437 out by the last curb by the stop sign facing west toward the interstate.

"Come on, 437," I'd say. "Come on." And I'd gently pull and turn her around. And I'd push her back across the Lot and park her squeezed in the middle of a row between a number of sleeping carts. "That oughta keep you out of trouble," I'd say. The next morning Cart 437 would be out by Garden Shop next to a plastic wheelbarrow facing west.

Dell, the Assistant Night Manager (aren't they almost always named Dell?), he said he'd been watching me and he liked my work and I could look forward to a 5 cent per hour raise after six months. That's 40 cents over an eight-hour day. That's big bucks if it's 1932. Of course, the Mart never hardly had to hand out those big raises—most cart wranglers only last two, three months at the most. But me, it wasn't about the money. I was prepared to hang on as long as it took.

In the spring I caught up with Cart 437 over by the Hy-Vee grocery store. Our parking lot connected with theirs. A number of our carts were pushed into the drainage ditches or shoved into the bushes along the side of the road. I found out that the bag boys and some of the produce kids from Hy-Vee were stealing my carts—joy-riding and abusing them. I went over there. I went over there on my time. I didn't care if I got paid. I didn't want to make a fuss. Me and the manager of Hy-Vee—we had words. He said, well, he didn't think it was any big deal—the kids playing with the Mart's carts—boys will be boys, they didn't mean nothing by it. I said rustling is rustling pure and simple. What was he going to do about it? He shrugged his shoulders. He smirked. Like political operatives smirk. Like fake moguls smirk. Like Emperor Nero—the original, the first smirker—smirked. I don't have time for smirkers.

I'm not a violent man, but I pulled out the pellet gun I got out of Sporting Goods and shot the Coke machine right next to him. Just to prove a point.

A few nights later I was bringing in a long line of carts from around the pharmacy entrance, and Dell (if they're not named Dell, they're named Don) said, could he have a word. I said I was busy, what did he need? He said, he wanted to give me a piece of advice—so this pasty overweight 28-year-old balding child with a logo of a two-bit rock band tattooed to his forearm was going to give me some advice. "Don't take this job so serious," he said.

I said, "Mister, I take everything serious." I was thinking about Cart 437. It had rolled somehow uphill around the corner across the street from the south exit. That's a quarter-mile or more as the crow flies. Didn't take a brain surgeon to figure Cart 437 was thinking about making a break.

Dell said he thought it might rain and did I know there was an opening for greeters? I said I didn't know nothing about that. I went back in the seasonal department and grabbed a banana and a raincoat and started to head on out. Got held up once again by Dell asking me if I knew anything about a goddamned Coke machine with a bullet in it. I said, I didn't know nothing about that neither. Then he made me sweep aisle nine. Then I went on after Cart 437.

It's been six days. Finally caught up with 437 at a Gas N' Go next to a strip mall a little west of Easton. At first I thought 437 must've got out on the highway somehow, rolling along the emergency lanes of the interstate to get this far out; but then I realized that the parking lot is like an unbroken inland sea—from the Mart to the malls to the mega malls spreading like fiords to the strip malls across the plains. You can get any way you want by going nowhere.

I lean on somebody's Ford for a moment. Light up a Marlboro. Flick the match into an oil stain at my feet. I figure this parking lot might just go all the way around the world. I got Cart 437 loaded up with Little Debbies and beer. I got an extra shirt. I figure we're going to have to return to the Mart eventually, but it's a cloudless day and we might just take the long way around.

Verifying Graffiti

1993

I CAN SEE YOU'RE AN INQUISITIVE SOUL. I can tell it's in your nature. You've been doing some serious thinking. You're willing to ask the tough questions. You can't help yourself. I hear things. I know you've been asking around—just exactly what are bridge abutments for?

It's a good question. It's pithy and to the point. And I'll give you the answer, but it's not as simple as it seems. We both know that we can toss out the pedestrian and obvious civil engineering company-line claptrap. Who cares who's supporting what? Bridge abutments are much more than a loosely affiliated pile of bricks and reinforced concrete. Come on. Here's the real deal.

Those rising towers are nothing more and nothing less than canvases for tortured and lonely souls who are trying to communicate with a harsh and beguiling world. So, when you see, as I have, the message "Doug Loves Judy" spray-painted in large, black and sure letters twenty-five, thirty-five, fifty-five feet above the ground, you'll know that you're witnessing more than a simple declarative sentence, more than a mere memorandum of puppy love. You're witnessing art. Art of the most exalted and highest nature.

It's always been thus. Every civilization, every piddly primitive tribe, every book club and every other contracted social situation in between have had one important aspect in common. They've always had some kind of municipal buildings and public structures on which to express themselves.

Take the classical Greeks. Right up there on the top tier of the Parthenon was spray-painted—in huge iridescent pink letters as large as life—"Paris Loves Helen." A little overwrought, perhaps. But, soul-searing nonetheless, and what about ancient Rome? Well, I can tell you for sure that at one time "Tony Loves Cleo" was delicately scrawled all over every marvelously engineered aqueduct from the Pyrenees to the Dead Sea. It's a fact. And if you peer back even further into the mists of time—you'll find "Ug ZugZug Erma" carefully etched on a load-bearing wall of some damp and Paleolithic cave just outside some ancient vineyard in the South of France.

But, you have to ask—are those towering, heartfelt words more than just paint on concrete? Well, yes. Are they impassioned? Yes, they are! Do they lend insight into the world around us? Obviously—yes! Without a doubt! But are the words true? One can only hope. One can only hope that those mad, lost visionaries with spray cans in their hands didn't crawl out on the slippery, wind-worn underbellies of some aqueduct or railroad trestle—just for advertising. No, you have to believe that when somebody screams out that they love somebody and they spell it out on a bridge—it's got to be the God's honest truth.

Of course, not all art is as bold and as assured as those messages of love. No, some of the writings show an anger and a passion and a shouting out against social injustice and moral bankruptcy heretofore unknown in the world of graphic representations.

Just on the other side of the bridge abutment that reads "Doug Loves Judy" are the wild and sneering words—"Central High Sucks." Again, there's no doubt that we are witnessing a vaunted form of self-expression. There is no doubt about the honorable artistic intent. But are those three simple words the naked, verifiable truth?

To find out I drove by Central High myself. Took fifteen, twenty minutes to find a parking spot. I walked in and walked down the long, forbidding halls. Got shouldered against a locker, got called names. Got my notebook slapped out of my hands. Got smacked in the back of the head with a dripping spitball. I ducked for cover into the school cafeteria, took a sniff, shuddered, swayed, and decided to forego lunch. I retreated.

But just as I was about to make my way out the door—an icy voice from behind called, "Where do you think you're going, young man?" And I said, "Nowhere in particular. I'm headed downtown to do a few things that need to be done before I head home to watch a bit of court TV and then a little local news. I like the parts about the weather." And the voice said, "Not so fast."

Little did I know, but I had been cornered and captured and was about to be interrogated by that most infamous and diabolical of all assistant vice principals known in the western world, Mrs. Bitenkruncher. We went back to her office. I asked if she could leave the door ajar. I offered alibis. I offered incentives. I pleaded my case from my knees. I broke down. I cried. We both cried. We discussed art. Anyway, the upshot is, I had to finish my lunch and was kept after class and forced to miss the big pep rally. I love pep rallies.

"Block that kick, block that kick, block that kick," et cetera.

So, to answer the question—does "Central High Suck"? Yes, it does. And what to do about it is simple.

Go to the game, sit with Doug and Judy, and root for the other team.

Your Mileage May Vary

2002

I GREW UP ON THE SOUTH SIDE of the largest pile of tires known to man. At its tallest the stack was the third highest peak in the state of California—higher than Mount Shasta and just slightly lower than Mount Whitney or Mount Williamson.

When the company found out that Old Radial was so high, they gave a big celebration with cable coverage, lite beer, and buffalo wings. The former mayor of San Luis Obispo gave a speech. But there was no music. We didn't need any. The mountain makes its own music. It creaks and calls. It sings sometimes down in the tunnels. And sometimes it's so silent, it's loud.

My Grandfather settled the eastern slope of the Pile (that's with a capital "P") with his young bride, Hanna; her sister, Sylvia; and Sylvia's shiftless common-law husband—Jammed Mike. They lived in a DT710 Radial—a big damned tractor tire. It could sleep six.

My dad and my oldest uncle moved next door into a 275 Forty R17 white sidewall when they were just little shavers.

My family's all over this mountain. Just last year, me, Anita, and little Jill leased a couple of oversized radials around the corner.

I'm a third-generation miner of valve stems and trace metals. It's okay work. Not much heavy lifting. It gets kind of dark and dirty sometimes. Sometimes it gets kinda tiring. Get it—tire-ing? Yeah, my wife doesn't think much of my sense of humor either.

I'm told snow falls and clings to the peak of Old Radial most of the year—even in July. But most of us don't really know the mountain from the outside. We see it from the inside. From the tunnels.

All those hundreds of millions of tires got crushed down and forced and pressured and compressed under their own weight to make natural passages with new tunnels being created all the time winding on for miles and miles in twisted and intricate strings. A guy could crawl anywhere in there. You get fast at it.

Dangerous though. 'Cause sometimes, more times than not, a few tires slip one by one and shift like bad discs in a spine, and a tunnel will get cut off and go nowhere and another will start up and make a new maze. When I was a kid, I lost my best friend, Lizzie, that way. A passage realigned and I heard her slip. I heard Lizzie holler, she said she was going to turn around and go back because that's all you could do. Maybe after a few days she came out into the sunlight on the other side of the mountain. Maybe she just kept having to follow the tunnels further into the depths. I think I hear her sometimes.

Then there's getting stuck. That's why the company favored children, short guys and skinny, thin-hipped women. That's why they called Jammed Mike, "Jammed Mike." He got his fat butt caught in every tunnel he ever crawled into. Never did make a quota.

I'm starting to sound like my old man—grousing and moaning about everything. It's not that bad. Not as bad as working the incinerators out in the Panamint Valley or having to pick through microwaves on the Appliance Range with their piles of VCRs and even higher and heavier stacks of refrigerators and ovens.

Don't get me wrong. I don't got nothing against the Appliance Range. Heck, good things come from all kinds of crazy places. Anita came off the Appliance Range. She wore earrings made of toaster springs and I loved her right off. She was slight and fast and she kissed me. I said, "You oughta come on over here and work the tire mines. You'd be good at it." She said she was good at a lot of things and I believed her.

She didn't smell like rubber. She'd grown up sleeping in the drum of a GE dryer with three separate fabric settings, so I guess sleeping in a tire with non-directional tread wasn't much of a change. We got married up at the Hotel Karaoke.

A guy once told me what tires were for. I told him I knew that. I'd heard of cars. You'd see them all the time down in the valley stripped of parts and rubber. I never gave them much thought.

Then a year or two ago the fires came and the mountain began to melt. A flow of oil, synthetics and steel spilled off the eastern rim and cut a serpentine cascade across the China Lake basin and poured into Death Valley. Filled the Valley about halfway up. Looked like a rubber ocean, if an ocean happens to look like the bottom of a shoe.

The company said there was still plenty of work to be done and the layoffs were due to unforeseen soft third-quarter, third-world demands and were just temporary. They said the heat in the tunnels was tolerable and was well within any nation's regulatory standards. I started thinking a lot about cars.

Jammed Mike sold me a 1960 Ford F-100 pickup truck he'd jury-rigged together. Two snow tires on the back, an all-weather dual-tread radial on the front right and an idiot wheel on the driver's side. But it runs and we're in it.

Anita's got little Jill on her lap and I'm driving. Funny to be rolling on what's left of the mountain. We're cutting north through Tonopah to give a wide berth to the Christian siege of Las Vegas. We're hoping to get over the Rockies before the heavy snows. Maybe head for the tire ridges outside Sioux Falls, wherever that is. I figure once a miner, always a miner.

Anita says she's not so sure. She could see us trying something new, something above ground. She smiles at the desert sky. She says, "Remember what the philosophers and warranties once foretold?" And I say, "What's that?" She opens up the glove compartment, pulls out a Firestone Tire and Rubber Company brochure and reads,

"Under-inflation or overloading may result in failure." She flips the page, "Your mileage may vary…"

I don't even know what mileage is, but I can see by the horizon up ahead, that "your mileage may vary" are words to live by.

The Slow Crossing

1994

THERE'S THIS PICTURE OF RICHARD IN MY MIND. He's in black, jeans and a T-shirt. The same black his brother always wore. He's with his brother. They're halfway across the street walking side by side and I've just waved and Richard has just nodded. He's learned from his brother, Bobby, that it's no longer cool to wave and say hi, you just give a quick bare nod. That's all that's necessary. I tried this on my mother and got slapped.

This is the last picture I have of Richard. This is the last time I saw him. I don't know about the first time I saw him. He came with the neighborhood and I came to the neighborhood before I can remember, way before kindergarten. We lived three houses away from each other. We played in the same sandbox. We always played Rat Patrol or cops and robbers. We wrapped ourselves in the branches of the weeping willow on the corner of Quincy and 17th Street and pretended that the headlights were searchlights and that if you were shined on you were shot. We always got shot. We always fell and rolled. We were students of slow, agonizing, slow-motion deaths, as seen on TV. We fell and died in the warm summer grass and talked. The headlights shone over us and finally we couldn't help it, we'd jump up and get shot again. What was the point in hiding?

Our main contribution to the world of American children at play in the early 1960s was to follow TV plots for our stories. We always called each other Bud. We always went up against incredible odds. Our wounds made us stronger. We lost in the beginning and won in the end. If we didn't have time to play out a whole episode, we played scenes from next week's show—that way we could skip all the stupid parts and get to the action. This is the way we always played, except when Bobby joined us. Then, he wanted to be the other side, he wanted to be the bad guy. And then, the robbers won. Me and Richard looked forward to being by ourselves.

One night Richard's mother sent the kids up to stay at our house. Their father was coming home. Usually when he came home, he was drunk. They were excited and talking. My father just wanted the kids to shut up and go to sleep. Richard's mother said don't worry, she'd handle it and she'd be back. My father hated aggravation. He called the police. The police came by, asked for a description of Richard's father, and said everything would be okay. Still, my father didn't let the kids go home until morning, after they'd gotten breakfast. Their pajamas always smelled of thick cigarette smoke. "Damnit, Sue, we're moving," my father said. "Don't curse in front of the children," my mother replied.

By that time Bobby was calling himself "Spider" and said he'd gotten recruited into a motorcycle gang, but not the Hells Angels, because the Hells Angels were sissies. He tattooed crosses on his arm with a blue ballpoint pen. He said the swastika was just an ancient backwards Indian sign. He was the born and sworn enemy to all teachers and police. He was twelve years old.

When I was eight or nine, right after my brother was born, we moved to a better neighborhood. I remember on the last few days before we left me and Richard sitting on the stoop and we'd take turns calling out the make and models of the cars that went by. Richard wasn't very good at it. He thought every car was a Chevrolet. I made the mistake of mixing up the act of not caring with being stupid. I don't remember saying good-bye to Richard. I just remember making a bad, lopsided trade with him—a full set of Batman cards (which are probably worth a million dollars) for a beat-to-shit Tonka truck (which I later smashed to pieces with a hammer).

In my mind there's this picture of Richard and Bobby. They're frozen in that picture. They're frozen halfway across the street like the Beatles in the Abbey Road album. And I know this is the way I'll always see them, frozen, held up, nowhere to go anyway. But I wish they'd take a few steps in that picture. I wish Richard would leave his brother and get out of the way. It's such a slow crossing and there are the headlights of a million Chevrolets coming up over the hill.

The Collapse of the Twentieth Century Was So Gradual

1997

THE COLLAPSE OF THE TWENTIETH CENTURY was so gradual.
The stuff that had been sent out into space came back.
And I'm not just talking about the debris, frozen waste, and capsules.
No, I'm talking about waves
    cosmic waves
    shock waves
    radio waves
    microwaves
    ultraviolet
    light itself—
    Every transmission, every beam from a flashlight shined at the stars by a bored Girl Scout, every signal, every campfire, every flick of a Zippo, every rerun of *I Love Lucy*—thousands and thousands of hours of Lucy
That's right, every broadcast of every TV show ever shown came reflected back from the heavens.
    Unviewed, unheard, unrated.
It was the return of memory
    the return of energy
    the return of light.
Naturally, both polar caps began to melt.
We, my daughter and I, were living in Greenland at the time,

because we wanted to watch the biggest ice cube in the world melt.
It did.
Now, the water laps biblically at our feet.
We keep the TV on to watch the shows return and rerun one last time backwards—"home I'm, Lucy."
We listen to the radio to hear the last backwards strains of Louis Armstrong, King Oliver, and whatever Alexander Graham Bell was supposed to have first muttered.
Then, it'll be a lot quieter.
The only waves of light and waves of sound will be from torches, gasses, and collapsing stars.
I don't know why the twentieth century fell in upon itself. Was it really that much thicker and more massive than any other?

The waters will recede—they always do.
And on the beach we, my daughter and I, will build a fire and shout at the sky.

Hoping the universe hears us in the next century.

The Secrets of Blackberry Pie

2011

WHEN I THINK OF MY MOTHER, I always think of pie. This may not sound all that mature or well-rounded, but it's how one boy thought. It's how my mother and I best communicated, I suppose. She baked and I ate whatever she baked with such relish and such joy that it made her smile.

My mother was the baker in her family. All the women cooked, of course. Everybody had to eat, so somebody was cooking something almost all the time, but in my mother's family they all believed they had their specialties. My mother's sister made tea and crocheted. Us kids had to wear the weird hats. My grandmother stirred up hot dishes that fed 300,000 church people in one sitting. These dishes always had little pieces of green pepper in them. It was left to us kids to pick them out.

And my mother baked, and seemingly only baked pies for me. I don't know what was wrong with the rest of my family. I don't know why my dad and my sister and my goofy little brother didn't love sweets the way I loved sweets. Sure, they ate cookies. They went to Dairy Queen. They acted like Americans. My dad even had a certain thing for Mars bars, but my family didn't understand pies. They didn't adore pie the way I did; the way pie was meant to be, must be, has to be worshipped.

Sometimes the pies, my pies, were given to and sampled by other people. Mrs. Butler, our next-door neighbor, got the occasional pie. The Stonewall Jackson Elementary School bake sale always got a few and I had to watch my pies be sold to the highest bidders.

It's not just my opinion that my mother's pies were wonderful. It was generally agreed that there was something special about my mother's pies.

"What's in those pies? They're so awfully good," the various usual people would ask.

"Nothing special," my mother would say.

"There's got to be a secret ingredient," they'd continue.

"I don't think so." My mother would smile and shake her head. Although, in retrospect, one did always have to wonder about the soup can of bacon grease that my mother kept under the sink at room temperature.

But, of course, there were secret ingredients.

Something in her half-Dutch heritage or maybe in her natural Depression-era austerity made my mother feel that her pies (well, any food actually) tasted better if the main ingredients were found for free. Why buy it, if you can pick it up off the ground?

My mother foraged in our neighborhood, which was actually easier than it sounds in the Washington, D.C. suburbs of the 1960s. You just had to know where to look. The apples for the apple pies came from an abandoned orchard up off 8th Street, which I think was the old Judge Thomas estate. The property is now a ring of dull row houses or, excuse me, executive townhomes.

The pears for the pear pies came from a branch of the McKann's pear tree that bent over our back fence. My mother claimed that any pear that dropped on her side of the line was hers by right and she could do with the pears what she would. God, those pies were incredible.

The berries for the blackberry pies came from along the railroad tracks. These blackberries—my mother always called them blackcaps (there being a difference in size and sweetness)—grew along the seldom-used Washington and Old Dominion Railroad right-of-way in Arlington County, Virginia, before the highways came through. There was a patch off the Harrison Street crossing and an even bigger and better patch below Wilson Boulevard on the other side of Four Mile Run.

The right kind of blackcaps apparently only grew along railroad tracks. They didn't grow along highways or sidewalks and especially didn't grow anywhere near Bon Air Park's prize-winning rose gardens. My mother would walk us down to see the American Beauties in bloom and we'd run around the rows like we were in a maze, but you could tell she'd just as soon be hunting for berries.

My mother tried a number of times, pretty much once or twice a season, to conscript us kids as berry pickers. You'd think with our pedigree and berry-eating bloodlines we would've been really, really good berry pickers, but we were really, really, really bad berry pickers. Mom would send us off into the dense June heat with one or two of her berry-stained berry baskets and we'd be back in 15 minutes exhausted having either picked the berries green or eaten what was left.

So my mother would huff, put on her giant yellow straw sun hat and go out and pick the berries herself and pick them correctly. She liked being down by the tracks anyway. They reminded her of being a kid, of following the tracks and waiting for her father at the station. But mostly, I think she just liked the smell of the ties, the dragonflies, and the breathless warmth of being alone along the rusted and ill-maintained tracks on a summer's day. She'd have denied it, but I saw her walking along balancing on one of the rails once.

But you're probably asking—what was the secret to the secret ingredient? What made the berries so much sweeter than regular berries?

It's hard to convey how incongruous Arlington County was to grow up in the 1960s. On the one hand, it literally overlooked the Nation's Capital. If you climbed a tall tree in my neighborhood you could see the Washington Monument. Yet, on the other hand, I remember horses and cows, vacant lots, woods, grass, and, of course, abandoned railroad beds: a complete lack of urban planning for what was to come.

Arlington was one of those nice little Southern places, a land that time forgot. But not for long. People were going to want to get to the big city and our town was in the way. Change was coming. Progress was bearing down.

My mother's reaction to change was to fight back, and there were two things she constantly fought when I was a kid: the highway coming through and her own mortality.

The first one was easy. While other people went to public zoning meetings or put anti-Interstate 66 signs in their yards, Mom waged a one-woman guerrilla campaign against the Virginia Highway Department. By that time, they'd torn up some of the tracks and left gashes in the woods, but there were still berries there and would be for a number of summers. Passing by the bulldozers and road graders on her way to pick what was left, my mother would calmly walk along on the dead red clay and calmly yank out a few surveyors' stakes. Sometimes she'd throw them into what was left of the woods. Sometimes she brought the stakes home and chucked them behind the garage.

As for death, she ignored it. She had lupus—basically she was allergic to her kidneys, her skin, to herself. So, she wore the sun hat, took those hideously large pills and never mentioned it to anyone.

Of course, I'm holding back on discussing the secret of the secret ingredient. What made those berries so perfect for pies? Was it the soil? The sun? Their natural hybrid vigor? There was something.

Usually, when asked what made her pies so special my mother would always say, "Oh, a little of this, a little of that." But once the President of the Clarendon African Violet Society pressed her and I heard the truth.

"Now, darling, do tell. You must tell. How come them berries are so sweet?"

"It's the creosote," my mother said.

"I beg your pardon?"

"It's the creosote. I believe it's probably a combination of dust, the angle of the sun, and the creosote on the ties that makes the berries taste like they do. They don't taste right otherwise."

The lady opted for just a small piece of pie. Good, more for me. She shouldn't have been eating my pie anyway.

It took seventeen years of legal injunctions, political battles, and federal and state territorial infighting before the highway actually plowed through the old neighborhood, making a two-block walk to the grocery store into a one-and-a-half mile, six-traffic-light slog; seventeen years from the time the Eisenhower administration decided to expand a one-track railroad into an eight-lane highway. 1959 to 1976.

One of the final images in my mind of my mother is her walking across the highway right-of-way with her sun hat and basket. She was thinner than ever and was wearing a goofy orthopedic device to protect the dialysis shunt on her ankle. She'd scoped out where the last berries were and was going to get them before the bulldozers did.

It's not often that a mother takes her son's advice. There's no reason for it. But one time I said, "Mom, you know, if you just keep pulling up the surveyor stakes and throwing them away the highway guys will just come along and put them back, but if you maybe just moved a couple of the stakes a few feet one way or another—maybe nobody would notice."

We ate the last of the blackberry pies in silence.

My mother's been dead a long time. She died well before the highway was completed.

But today, if you happen to be driving in the far right-hand, northbound lane of Interstate Route 66 towards D.C., somewhere between what used to be called Westover Field and the Harrison Street overpass, you might notice a slight little jiggy-joggy in the road where it feels like maybe the surveyors took one quick step to the left and then one quicker step back to the right, and all the traffic swerves and wobbles just a little bit going by at 65 miles per hour.

That's where the berries used to be.

I still like pie. I try to buy a slice of pie whenever and wherever I can: roadside diners, fancy restaurants, national franchises. All the pie seems to taste just about the same cardboardy same. There just seems to be something always missing in those recipes. Must be the creosote.

Clones Day Parade

2001

LIKE MANY OF YOU, I was on my way to the annual Clones Day Parade the other day. I was late. There was a clone in front me driving a van and he was late and there was a clone in front him driving a van and he was late and there was a clone behind me driving a van and she was late. The road looked like the reflection you'd find in a box of mirrors—clones and roads as far as the eye could see.

We were all late. And it wasn't getting any earlier, if you know what I mean.

So, I leaned out my window and hollered to the girl clone driving the SUV next to me—I said, "Hey, girl clone—since things have sort of slowed down, how about you and me getting together and making a bunch a little baby clones?" She explained to me that you don't need two to make a clone and then she told me in very explicit language just exactly what I needed to do, to do what I proposed.

She drove off and hit the van in front of her and that van hit the van in front of it, which hit the van in front of it which hit the van in front—well, you remember our discussion about the box of mirrors.

It seemed to me if I was going to make it to the Clones Day Parade before doomsday I was going to have to get clever and think of something quick. But as I was a clone—so I thought like a clone. And when I pulled out into the emergency-only lane to drive past all my brother clones—all the other clones had already pulled out to drive by their brother clones. So, I pulled back in my own lane and all the other clones did the same thing. So, I swerved into the emergency lane again—

—that wasn't going to work. I felt myself getting all balled up into a pretty good early-morning case of drive-time road rage.

I put the pedal to the metal in my clone mobile and roared past a million others. I went sixty. I went seventy. I went ninety. I ran a red light. I ran an orange light. I ran a whole bunch of yellow lights. I pumped my fist and screamed from behind the wheel.

And just as I thought I was making headway I went full circle and came plowing up—right behind time. Just rammed right into it. It wasn't pretty. Being stuck behind time. There's a lot of time to get stuck behind.

So, there I was—trying to pass time. It took three and a half billion years to get by the mud and ash of the Precambrian period. All that did for me was to get me stuck in line behind two trillion trilobites crawling along what would become the Santa Monica Freeway.

Stopped for gas in the Devonian period. The guy taking the cash was one of the original fish—the ones with true and translucent scales. He crawled out of a puddle and cleaned my windshield. Gave me some trading stamps.

Pulled off for a bite to eat at the Permian cafe located somewhere in west Texas. The waitress was a cute stegosaurus. She smiled and chewed gum. Showed me a picture of her kids. Told me she got off at ten. She got the order wrong. Everything took forever. By the time I got a refill on the coffee and finally got my piece of pie two out of three of the customers were extinct.

I felt kind of lonely. I played with a little package of sugar and glanced out the plate-glass window and saw another lonely clone looking at me and he saw a lonely clone looking at him and that one saw a lonely clone looking at—it was like being in a box of mirrors with an ashtray on each table.

Got back in the van—evolution pulled up beside me weaving all over the place. Wasn't paying one bit of attention to where it was going. Took a left turn from the right-turn-only lane. Cut me off. It rolled down its driver's side tinted window and offered me an opposable thumb, a bigger brainpan, and a prehensile tail. Said I could only keep two. I'm still wondering if I shouldn't've opted for the big fuzzy tail.

I rolled on and passed the Pleistocene like it was standing still. The glaciers receded and the rains came. Luckily I was driving on all-weather tires.

Entered the tiny era of human dominion. And boy, then the centuries really got clogged up with crap—gears and obelisks and the many dismal philosophies. Here's a couple words of advice—judge no clone by the pottery they make. And don't bother reading what's written on the monuments.

I was getting close. I could smell it. I pushed and shoved between the centuries. Passing the sixteenth. Passing the seventeenth.

Got stuck behind the twentieth. I flashed my lights. I honked. That century just smiled, stayed in the way, weaved around a little. Made me mad. I swung out across the double yellow lines and plowed my way toward the oncoming headlights going right on by. I held my breath. I dove back into my own lane just in time to get caught behind yet another century. I guess I'd passed just about as much time as I could.

Out of the corner of my eye I can see a million, billion clones. I now know we all came across the desert of time together. We'd all had similar experiences eating pie at the Permian Cafe. Now, we have caught up. This is our century.

There will be no more Mondays or Sundays. Every day will be Clones Day. Out of test tubes and the wells of Petri dishes we will strap on our rollerblades and climb into our vans. We will march in the annual Clones Day Parade, which, by the way, will be held daily.

Clones on the open road. Clones in formation. Clones scouting the perimeter.

We will take in the sights of the centuries to come. We will continue to meet ourselves in the box of mirrors. And like the trilobites before us—we will march until we turn to stone.

The New Silence

2019

BRIAN PRICE

The New Silence

Silence is coming.
It'll be a new silence. That's what they say.
I don't know what this silence will sound like.
I don't think I've ever known real silence,
But it's coming.

Before it gets silent it'll get loud.
These changes—they'll be loud.
The rain will be like tons of loose gravel falling from the sky.
The ice will splinter and fail and howl.
The waves will rage.
The wind will take and want and want.

I promise to do what I can—what do you need? Five bucks, ten bucks?
Whales. Everybody likes whales. Maybe we should give the money
directly to the whales—let them use the money for what they need.
We'll go all in. Stop flushing the toilet. Eat Brussels sprouts.
Do whatever it takes. I'll mend my ways. I'll make a sacrifice.

I heard that
If you laid all the green lawns in the United States
End to end, well, not end to end
But maybe like a patchwork quilt.
If you gathered them together, all the zoysia, the bluegrass, the weeds
and the creeping Charlie, if you laid them all together like a puzzle
They would be the size of Texas.
Every week America mows Texas.
I know it feels like it. It feels like I mow Texas every week.

That's it—that will be my sacrifice—the earth can have my lawn.
The climate can have it back. Here is my lawn. I don't need it that bad.

But what shall it become? What shall it become?
When it is very very quiet,
When it is so silent,
What shall it become, dear Marjorie, what shall it become?

The Land

I want to be part of the land
Not on it
Not tending, not plowing, not mowing,
Not grazing, not picking, not improving.

I want to need the land
Like a snapping turtle needs the sand to burrow
Like a skunk needs the woodpile behind the shed
Like all those insects that appear and have disappeared.

I want the land to need me
This is the tough part
I want the woods to say our shadow is your shadow
It's deeper that way
It's darker that way
The shadow works better with both of us in it.

I would say that I would choose the woods
That's what I want to say, that's what I'd like to say
They look so comfortable, dappled and diffused
I'd follow the paths or what appear to be paths
It'd be safe, it'd be ok
We can go in—
But like Hansel, if he wouldn't have been egged on by Gretel,
I'm just not ready.

Out of Africa

After wandering around in the woods for a while
I see a piece of sky at the end of a dense path.
I'm drawn towards that door of light.
I stand up,
I'm only human,
And I want to be the tallest thing on the savannah.

The Gate

That door out of your bedroom
Into the back yard,
I wanted one of those doors.
I wanted one that you could drive a truck through,
I wanted to escape that bad,
And I don't know why,
Because I just turned around and bought a house
That desperately needs a secret door from the bedroom to the back yard.

The front lawn out front is like a moat,
Lifeless in its protection.
Mormons and siding salesmen bang at the gate
And moths die in the lights.
Back in the dark ages,
They used to set the moat on fire to defend the castle.
That seems kind of extreme, but maybe not.

We gaze out your window out back
And say, we could cross that.
Even on our knees, even on all fours,
We could cross the lawn.
Past the grubs, past the moles,
Following the paths that the hedgehogs make.
We wouldn't starve, we wouldn't dehydrate,
We wouldn't forget what we were doing.

The goal would be to get to the fence,
To find a hole in it, to stare even just two feet beyond it,

Where decisions would have to be made.
We all know about the secret door.
We all know it is a way out.
But what, dear Marjorie, what would you let in?

The Hose and the Sandbox

At the end of the summer, my mother would let us flood the sandbox.
Usually we weren't allowed to play with the hose,
Because, you know, things would get out of hand.
But once a summer we'd get to drag the green and kinked garden hose across the lawn and get ready—
We'd been getting ready for a couple of weeks, maybe a month.

Me and my best friend Richard had dug intricate tunnels and piled up a pile of sand that was going to be a volcano. We built a spiral of walls up the sides and made places for plastic army men to hide. You could drive a Jeep all the way up to the top. But first you had to stop at the popsicle gate manned by more plastic army men. Richard had gotten a whole bag of green army men for Christmas.

We had roads crisscrossing everywhere for the tanks and half-tracks,
And bridges and arches,
And telephone poles made from twigs.
We molded different sized towers out of cottage cheese containers and Dixie cups. They had sticks for guns and we poked windows in the sandy walls with our pinkies.

Then we dug a canal, because if we were going to have real water you'd need a real canal. We folded up a couple of paper boats.
There was no castle. This was no beach.

It was the back yard and it was going to look so real. Our little town and the army base and the plastic cars and plastic men were going to look so real, and they did look so real, as real as TV.

Richard held the hose and I twisted on the spigot on the side of the house.
I stopped to unkink a few kinks, and ran as fast as I could to see the first dribbles of water fill up the canal and then turn into a river that roared under the bridges and then over the bridges and drown twelve matchbox cars.

The tanks sank.
The popsicle gate floated away.
One tower cracked and then collapsed and then another.
We let the water rush down the side of the volcano like it was lava.

It happened so fast. That entire world turned into mud. Our hands were filthy and our pants were soaked. We just barely made it out alive.

Who knew that the same thing would happen to Cincinnati in 2032?

Somehow

Somehow they got it all mixed up
And they turned wine into water
They took a giant leap that became a small step
They found a tunnel at the end of the light
They made a molehill out of a mountain

Somehow they got it all mixed up
And spoke power to truth
And that's how whatever happened happened.

Adaptation

In the near future when the world is a desert and is drowning at the same time, there will be new rules.
What once was will no longer be necessary or enough.
We will have to adapt, all of us will. All of us—will have to adapt.

Nature should have known this. Nature should have been prepared.
Because it only stands to reason that nature will have to adapt more and quicker than the rest of us. Nature will have to do the unthinkable.
Nature will have to become more human.

Skunks will have to learn to smell like gasoline.
Elephants will have to act like trucks.
Whales will be submarines.
And insects will imitate legos.

To survive in the new climate we all will have to use the same old tricks.
Camouflage and mimicry, modification and, of course, procreation.

Geese will sound like traffic.
Sloths will learn to tick like clocks.
Bees will constantly buzz like refrigerators.
And locusts will sound like, well, probably sound like locusts. That's not a good example. What I'm trying to say is—to truly survive in the new climate, nature will have to learn to sound—electric.

Frogs will impersonate car alarms.
Flies will mimic cell phones.
Wolves will howl like sirens.
Everything in the new climate will sound like an emergency.

The Last Ones

I met the last giraffe.
She had sad soulful eyes.
She stood over a fallen tree.
She no longer had to be tall.

I met the last cricket.
He was hiding behind the garage door.
His name wasn't Jiminy.
I think it was Doug.

I met the last butterfly.
I rode it like a horse.
We went to the moon.
It wasn't far enough.

The Evil Word

Shall we talk about the evil “E” word?
We all know the evil “E” word.
Of course we do.
Then what is it?
Say it.
Extinction?
No, economics.

The Day After the Election

When the oceans are half plastic
When Texas catches fire
When the winds never calm
    Will we be able to find each other?
I don't want to lose track. Losing track of you would be like losing track of myself.

There will be a day (I'm not saying when but maybe soon) when the earth's rotation will slow down. The day after that the earth will wobble and I'm not saying I understand the physics, but the earth will stop and then start and then spin in the other direction.

You may feel a little nauseous, maybe a little light-headed. Your refrigerator magnets will fall to the floor. The usual will happen—your phone's battery will go dead. This will be bad, because we'll want to talk.
We'll want to meet. Perhaps we'll want to kiss.

When the rivers smolder
When California slips into the sea (oh, where's Steely Dan when you need them?)
When you can't find the back yard for all the smoke and fumes
When our masks fall away,

I will love you
I will love you
I will love you even when we can't breathe.

Prayers

The Gods who rule the new silences will be ancient gods,
As they have always been. They will continue to wait for us in emerald glades. Their whispers will mingle with the leaves and styrofoam cups that blow across the street. Their thumbs will press upon our scales.

Our prayers will remain the ancient prayers:
Please, please, Tiger Tiger, please do not eat me.
Please, please, rotting corn, please feed me.
Please, please, pestilence, take my neighbor first.
Please, car, please—start just one more time.

Oh, Digital Nymph, please, please save what I forgot to save. Please put it back the way it was before I lost it.
I will be good next time. I will hit the control button. I will not hit Control-Alt-Delete. I will press F-1 repeatedly. I will back up.
I will do whatever it is that I think you think you want me to do.

Those who do not believe in you don't really mean it.
They'll believe in you when their keys fall down between the iron slats of a sewer grate.
They'll believe in you when they think they've heard their mother's voices call for them.
They know that you control the rains.
They know that you know where their sunglasses are.
They know that you influence all arrivals and departures.
They believe in the sacraments of inconvenience.

I will shout your praises from the tops of muddy hillocks.

I will stand waist-deep in wet cardboard.
I will remind all of the modern souls of the ancient floods.
I will say what we all would say,
"Get me out of here."
The Golden Bough will bow down and dip into the rising waters.

Invitations

They have gone.
The noisy nests, the holes, the nooks, the spaces under the stairs.
They're empty.
The Passenger Pigeon, the Western Black Rhino, the Wooly Mammoth.
Some spaces have been empty for years.

The powders and the poisons,
And the ash—all that ash—they couldn't breathe.
Of course, neither can we, but that's the choice we've made, or the choice made for us. I hate that word, "choice." It always makes it sound like we had one.
But there will be one choice we'll have to make.
This will sound cute and trite and not at all understanding of how things really work in a, you know, corporate way, but we'll have to invite them back.
We may have to go from empty nest to empty nest, from hole to hole, shake paws and rub elbows with snouts,
Hand out flyers and invite them to public meetings.
We'll have to say we're sorry.
We'll have to say we didn't mean it.

It does work. A few summers ago I found a few pods of milkweed and let them blow across the yard. A couple stalks came up and then the next summer a couple more. This summer there were a dozen and I saw two monarch butterflies. They came back. It does work.

We'll invite them all. We'll invite every one.
We'll invite them all back.

But if they do come back,
Will they be ghosts?

Fish Concerns

1993

The sea has no center. There is no one place any more representative than any other place under the waves. You must go and arrive and arrive. So, you walk in up to your knees, up to your chest, over your best judgment looking for fish. Or maybe you hang over the side of the boat retching, hoping for glimpses. There's something there, a refracted shadow or some bent motion. It seems familiar or perhaps it seems like something you ought to know. In that darkness and in that dazed softness there must be secrets. We all love secrets, especially about ourselves and the fins we once had.

Let's discuss Peter and other fishermen of men. Like most men, Peter and his ilk are looking for a woman just like dear old Mom. And like most men they really don't know that much about their mothers. What was she wearing last? What did she dream? Why did she cry silently to herself when she served tuna? Peter doesn't know. He gulped down his chowder and banged out the door, almost forgetting his rod and reel. How was the fishing? Well, Peter caught one and threw him back in. The next guy caught one and threw him back. The man in the faded waders caught one and threw him back in. So, it can be safely assumed that there is only one soul in the sea and it's under the limit.

I met a mermaid, well, actually, a close friend of mine met a mermaid and he told me this true story. He said the mermaid knew some secrets, especially about ourselves and the fins we once had, and she wanted to know if he wanted to know. He said, "Sure, of course." So, she invited him in, but only for a minute, because her parents weren't home. Her father, Neptune, was in the Gulf, raging, and her mother, the Moon, was waning. "Nice place," my close friend said, pointing to the coral beds, bald radial tires, and algae. "We like it," she replied. Coy conversation and wet kisses. And the noise—fish are loud, especially carp and blowfish, while sharks are the strong silent types. Of course, my close friend knew all this, being somewhat of an ichthyologist. However, there was one thing he had to know. One question he had to ask. It was the question that would tie Atlantis to the Titanic, Captain Ahab to Jacques Cousteau, and perhaps the great killer boss wave to Pismo Beach. He hemmed. He hawed. She tugged on his zipper and fingered his bright buttons—trinkets that attract so many mermaids. He looked around, a little self-conscious, and asked, "Hey, where is your undersea kingdom?" She shrugged, shy and surprised, annoyed and answered, "There is no undersea kingdom, what do you expect from fish?"

The other night the president came on TV and announced that he'd decided to appoint a fish (probably a member of the popular Osteichthyes family) as Secretary of the Navy. The news was met with the usual cheers ("We're so pleased and wish nothing but the best for our scaly underwater friends everywhere."), resentment ("It's about time!"), and disbelief ("But don't we already have the Sturgeon General?"). Insects demanded equal rights and got a grasshopper named to the National Farm Defoliation Council. And rightfully so.

Evidence and fossils of fish abound on the plains and in the mountains. Once the world was totally under water. Once everything was a secret under the waves. But for some, possibly once is not enough. Once is not proof of supremacy.

After all, as a largemouth bass once put it to me—
When it rains, shouldn't fish be in the sky?

Hard Hops and Perfect Surfaces

1995

YOU'RE STANDING NEXT TO YOUR CAR fumbling for your keys.

A baseball rolls by.

You wonder if this is unusual or is this just the way it is when the world is connected more and more by hard flat surfaces?

You don't follow the ball. You look back to where you think the ball came from. There's a high fence and an open hole where the gate used to be. There's a wall and a church just beyond. And caught in the enclosure they create are uniformed kids screaming and chattering and doing whatever kids do.

For a moment you lean against the pole of a bent and chainless basketball hoop and think about little victories.

In the city, almost all institutions are built on tar, set in and surrounded by tar. The unbroken, black plain spreads from the commercial to the municipal. But, by far, the hardest surfaces are found in the parochial. I'm talking about Catholic schools: St. Ann's, St. Agnes, St. Catherine's, St. Stephen's—the lonely patron of the Grateful Dead—the list goes on and on and spreads across the land.

This is the way it goes. Good Catholics send their Catholic kids to Catholic schools. And rightfully so. And though these schools do their jobs and serve their God, there is one ugly stained statistic that stands out above all others. At these parochial schools, built on and molded to tar, there are more torn knees and bloodied elbows per attending child than on any other sample group at any other sample temple of learning in any other sample neighborhood on any other sample planet in any other sample universe known to man.

These playgrounds are dangerous, hard, unforgiving places. But those kids have to play somewhere. What do you expect of a bunch of five- to twelve-year-olds running as fast as they can—in blazers and matching navy slacks for the boys and those devastatingly stylish plaid shirts for the girls. Oh, those skirts and my little boy, public-school Protestant fantasies of pink knees and all that they led to. What do you expect? They have to play somewhere.

The nuns line them up for kickball and four square—the bases and lines painted unevenly on the patched asphalt. The balls bounce high and viciously—the games are quick and sharp. The left field wall may almost be too close, similar to Fenway. And it's tricky—a looping line drive off the windowed brick wall of the rectory can go for extra bases, and a hard smash off the bottom of the wall can maim or, at least, confuse an outfielder. But, a broken window on the same wall ain't exactly a home run in this league. A broken window may mean status among your peers, but it also may mean detention or writing some saint's name on the blackboard 500 times. These games don't tend to be pitchers' duels. They're more like playing baseball inside a pinball machine. 47 to 44 is a typical score—and that's only after the first inning.

You may be wondering how I know all this. Well, I lived across the street from the Sullivans and the O'Malleys. I got shoved to the ground regularly by Danny DiPenti. He'd sit on my chest and ask me if I loved his sister. I'd say, "No." He'd say, "What?" And I'd say, "No." He'd say, "What?" and grind his knees into my skinny ribs. "Yes," I'd say, "Okay, okay, yes, get off." What wasn't there to love? Theresa Marie wore blue-rhinestone glasses and was even shorter than me. She had a bright, exotic overbite. She had skinned knees and I'd stop, hang on the fence and watch them play on my way to school. Theresa Marie would look over her shoulder, turn, and jump and wave. She had a silly, beautiful way of having no idea what was going on around her. One time Stevie, another one of her many brothers, yanked a high inside fastball down the right field line, just missing Theresa Marie's ear and shattering a barred first floor rectory window—the perfect shot. The kids swirled and circled the blacktop like a flock of starlings. I ran too, and I don't even know why. Theresa Marie tripped and skinned an old scab off.

Of course, the asphalt wasn't meant for the children at all. No. All that tar, all that beautiful smooth surface was for Sundays and Wednesday nights, for worship. Those city Catholics teetering on the far end of a threadbare diocese had to conserve space. They had to use their property for more than one purpose at a time. The property had to multitask, and offering free and convenient parking to the parish was high up on the list. For a few hours each Sunday cars sat silently between the lines painted especially for them, and the kids were inside squirming in the pews.

But during the week, the parking lot was a battleground. We used to walk by and watch them through the 12-foot-high fences and maybe throw a few rocks. The Sullivans and DiPentis threw back and then went back to battling themselves. They ran out routine pop flies and slid into second. They played for keeps. They played for loose teeth and scabs of honor. They played hurt. The nuns called a pretty strict game and had narrow strike zones. Every now and then one would sweep some broken glass off the base path with a dark and hidden foot.

It is my belief that those playing surfaces were the precursors to AstroTurf—low maintenance, all-weather, more debilitating injuries. You have to wonder, if it wasn't Sister Mary Innocence—a crazed, limping, one-eyed junior high school gym-teaching nun and not some multi-million dollar athletic program at Notre Dame—who invented the turf. The perfect surface, God-given, perfect hops.

A few weeds still grow in the cracks where the school meets the parking lot—most likely a Catholic kid's only run-in with plant life before they got sent off to camp.

All in all, these kids, these tough and scarred Catholics, probably ended up better prepared for life on the paved expanses of our world than most of their Protestant, soft suburban neighbors who played in the green muddy fields of the public schools just down the block. We only fought bees and dog turds. Those Catholic kids understood the geometry of hard surfaces and accepted the reality that only heavy traffic can change the course of a rolling object.

One time I was alone. That's the only way you could watch for long, and John O'Malley cracked a ball over the fence. It banged off the hood of the Oldsmobile right behind me. I froze. The ball rolled out in the street, spun back, and rolled under a parked truck into a puddle. I went and reached under there as far as I could and I just could barely get the ball. All the kids were hollering for me to give it, for me to throw it back. Theresa Marie was at the fence and I went up and I tried to hand it through to her, but like all fences the holes weren't quite big enough for a baseball. Our hands brushed when we were trying to get the ball through. Her hand was smooth and alive. Mine smelled like street oil and gutter dirt. I itched my nose with the dirtier one. I wanted to tell her something, but I couldn't think of anything. Theresa Marie told me, "Ah, just go ahead and chuck it." I stepped back a couple of steps to get a running start. I threw that ball as hard and as far as I could—a one-hopper right to the pitcher—a perfect hop, a perfect throw. Danny gave me a cool nod and I only nodded back and then I ran home. It was the proudest moment of my life.

In these times, of course, those small asphalt playgrounds just feed into the greater lots of the malls and the industrial parks and there are moments when a hard skipping grounder will take a bad hop, slide past a shortstop, accelerate between the right and center fielders through the hole in the fence where the gate used to be and roll and roll on and on forever.

And so it is with this baseball that has just rolled by you—it keeps on skipping along, missing the tires of abandoned cars, going between legs and the wheels of shopping carts, and jumping curbs until it becomes a dot on the horizon. You wonder if you shouldn't be trying to chase it down, so you can throw it back.

The Hill

2005

MAJOR JAMES R. O'CONNOR, Jr., ret. died a few years back. I was in town visiting my mother and she suggested we should go to the funeral.

"You knew him, Danny. We need to go and pay our respects," she said, putting on a red plaid woolen scarf that made her look ten years older or at least ten years behind the times.

"I knew him when I was like fourteen or fifteen," I said.

"That counts."

"I never hardly talked to him."

"I imagine Kim will be there."

We missed the funeral. That was probably by design. My mother doesn't like funerals. But she feels obligated. She always feels obligated.

The reception was at the O'Connor's house, which was easy enough to find, because it was around the corner, kind of, from where we used to live. I say kind of because that neighborhood had a number of streets that dead-ended around a gully that led into some woods that surrounded a storm-sewer kind-of creek that led into a highway right-of-way. I used to slip out the back door, cut across our sloping side yard, jump the trampled fence, get scratched by a few briars, balance on the boards across the creek and end up at Kim's sliding back door in a couple of minutes. It took a lot longer to drive to Kim's house, take a right and then another right, which actually curved left like the gully and then finally take another right to the end of the cul-de-sac.

The O'Connor's house looked about the same—light blue—just like it was six or seven years before when I'd known it. I gave my mother my arm as we walked up the rain-slick brick walkway. We had our collars up.

The front door was ajar. Nobody answered our knock, so we just went in. I didn't see anybody I knew, which was a relief. I don't know if I'd ever been through the front door before. I'd always gone in around back.

I let my mother disappear into a crowd of churchwomen in the entryway. I kept my coat on and wandered into the kitchen. The kitchen I did know. That was my territory. When we were kids we were always sneaking up to the kitchen.

There were half-dug-into Tupperware and plastic-wrapped dishes of Jell-O and baked beans, lima beans, bean salad, and bean dip on the counters. There were empty platters in the sink and more stacked up on the stove. I just wanted a glass of water, but you couldn't quite get a glass up under the faucet because there was so much stuff stacked up in the sink. I turned it on anyway and the water ricocheted off the dirty plates all over the front of me. I looked around for a dish towel or a rag and there was one draped over the doorknob of the door to the basement.

The basement. Kim's mother called it the rec room. Her father called it his den. I called it a basement just to bug Kim.

"It's not a basement. It's like a family multi-purpose room," Kim used to explain before she knew she'd been played for a sucker and hit a ping-pong ball as hard as she could at me.

"What, like the school gym?"

"You're such a stoop," Kim would say with a gentleness in her eyes. The only other person she called "a stoop" was her brother.

Her older brother, Jimmy (there were just the two kids), had made the basement into what it was, or what it became. He'd made the big improvements—a single bed walled off by a row of filing cabinets and metal shelves, a three-legged comfy chair and a listing couch, a record player with an old middle for 45s, a coat hanger rod hanging from exposed pipes on the ceiling, and a series of tie-dye sheets to wall off the laundry room. He'd rolled the lawn mower outside, so you didn't have to trip over it at night. He almost always used the glass sliding door to go in and out. Then he went to college.

So, Kim inherited the territory, moving out of her pink and Barbie bedroom and spending more and more time downstairs. She put up posters of Cream and Jimi Hendrix even though she was just around eleven when Jimi died. She had her brother's taste in music.

When we were fifteen that one summer we did a lot of hanging out in Kim's basement. Peter Meyers, Wendy and Katie Salander, Kim and me. We were inseparable, for a while anyway. We were lazy, couldn't drive, and not much was asked of us. We were teenagers.

That's what I was thinking when I turned the knob of the basement door, glanced around hoping nobody was looking, and started to descend.

"You live in my basement?"

"Huh?" I said. I jumped about fifteen feet into the air. I'd been sent up by Kim to the kitchen to get some potato chips. The Major was between me and the door.

"I asked you a question."

"Ah, no…"

"I think you do. I think you live in my basement."

"No, really, I… I…"

"I ought to charge you rent." The Major half-smiled. He let me by. I was so grateful. I didn't even know who he was.

Major O'Connor had come home in the middle of the summer toward the end of June. He was back again from Vietnam. He'd been there a mess of times.

He slept, mostly—either up in the master bedroom with the window air conditioner blasting away or in the leather easy chair in front of the TV. You might hear a door click shut or click open. Sometimes you'd hear footsteps up above, the toilet flush, the shades being drawn; but mostly you didn't hear anything and you hoped it would stay that way.

"Kimmie, get your hair out of your eyes. And remember to make sure your father gets his medicine," was about all Mrs. O'Connor ever said to Kim. She had a white-gloved, leopard-skin-pill-box-hat Jackie Kennedy kind of look about her. She was sort of stuck in that era, or at least that's what my mother said.

She sold real estate and was always leaving unread messages on the refrigerator. She never came downstairs, not even to do laundry. That was left up to Kim. The basement always smelled like laundry. I kind of liked that smell. I still like the smell of laundry. "You could be so pretty," Kim's mother would take a glossy-red-nailed pinky and try to tuck a lock of Kim's blond hair behind an ear. Kim would duck away and head for the basement. I thought Kim looked like Peggy Lipton of the Mod Squad. I thought she was the most beautiful girl in the world.

Kim and I first met when we were just turning 12 just after 6th grade just before junior high. I was cutting through her back yard. It was towards the end of summer. The O'Connors had just moved in. I was humming. God, can you believe that, I was humming. She came completely out of nowhere and scared the hell out of me.

"Where you going?" she asked.

I looked around. "Home," I said.

"What? You live in the woods?"

"I wish."

I showed Kim most of my world that day—the one clear pool in the creek, the four boards that made the bridge, the climbing tree, and the path to the highway that you weren't supposed to take. I told her my dad was never home and she said hers wasn't either.

We played together almost all the time for a while, ping-pong and the

"What do you wanna do? I don't know, what do you wanna do?" kind of stuff, and then it rained or she got sent off to an aunt. I forget which and it might've been both.

Anyway, it was about Labor Day before I saw her again. I was coming out of the woods cutting up the hill of her back yard. Probably going to Pete's, that's what I was usually doing. Kim just appeared in front of me. She was just there. She was always doing that. She didn't say anything. She stood in my way halfway up the hill. I didn't say anything either and veered left to go around her. She stood in my way. So, I stopped and then started right. She moved and stood in my way. I stopped again, leaned left and then tried to sprint an end around. She pushed me and I slipped a little. I got my footing, faked and tried again. She caught me like a linebacker and we both went rolling down the hill of zoysia grass—prickly and soft at the same time. We ended up with her sitting on my chest trying to pin my wrists to the ground. I wiggled and bucked her off and took off once again up the hill. She barely caught my ankle and I landed flat on my face. She tried to run by me to reclaim the higher ground and I grabbed her ankle and held on and pulled. We went rolling back down the hill again, her ending up on my chest again, trying to pin my wrists to the ground again. I bucked and fought and we wrestled. We got up yanking and grabbing. She caught me by one wrist with both hands and swung me 'round as hard as she could and I went flying. I got up, grabbed her by a wrist and did the same thing and she went flying. It was almost fun, but it wasn't. It was like a war. Neither of us got anywhere. Neither of us could make it to the top of the hill without being tackled by the other and sliding and rolling down in a pile to the bottom again. We went on forever until neither of us could hardly stand up.

We finally fell over and lay there side by side on the side of the hill, smudged and grass-stained, breathing hard under the warm, quiet sky. There was grass in my left ear. My pant knees were torn and I had a bloodied elbow. Kim had a bit lip and her hair was tangled across her face with bits of blond straw sticking out. We lay there a long time, long enough to put our hands behind our heads and watch the clouds. We never said a word. Her mother called. Kim leaned on one elbow, kissed my forehead and ran up the hill.

I lay there almost 'til dark, until I finally went back home, because I couldn't remember where I was headed in the first place.

School started a day or two later and for the next three years I seldom saw Kim, maybe a time or two, maybe with other kids. But we went to different junior highs. Me to public school. Her to the Catholic school on the other end of town. I sometimes cut through her back yard just to see if she'd come out.

The ping-pong table is the first thing you see when you go down the stairs or come through the sliding glass back door to the O'Connor's den. Either way. The table almost always had a box or a hamper on it that you had to move to play. When I went down during the funeral reception there was a box of books and files sitting on the table. I set them off to the side. I found some ping-pong paddles on a metal shelf covered in cobwebs leaning on a dented ping-pong ball. I took the ball and a cracked and taped paddle and mindlessly kept the ball bobbing. It was something I did a lot that summer in Kim's father's den.

"Kind of hard to play ping-pong by yourself, isn't it?"

That was the first thing Kim's father ever said to me. He'd appeared out of nowhere, which was the way he usually appeared. I was alone in the basement waiting for Kim and the twins. A lot of times I'd come over and there'd be nobody there. They'd be over at a party or something, but I'd hang around anyway, bopping a ping-pong ball and watching fuzzy gray TV, hanging around like the bald snow tire that leaned against the furnace.

Sometimes, I'd fall asleep on the lopsided couch. Kim would come home from wherever she'd been and throw a blanket over me. "You're such a stoop," she'd say. She asked me how come my mom didn't worry.

I told her that I'd told my mom that it wasn't that I didn't come home; it was that I left real early. I told her I had a paper route.

The Major looked at me like he was looking into a pool for something he could recognize, but the ripples kept getting in the way.

"I just try to keep bopping it," I said and I tried to hand him the ping-pong paddle because that's what I thought I was supposed to do.

He waved it away and wandered over to the snow tire and kicked it. "Don't hurt yourself," he said and drifted back upstairs.

Ping-pong was pretty much the only game we played down in the basement. Five-handed ping-pong and smoking the little bit of weed that Peter could steal from his brother. And smoking cigarettes to cover up the dope smoke, and drinking the weird concoctions Wendy and Katie mixed together from their parents' liquor cabinet.

My once best friend, Peter Meyers, who was just getting weirder and weirder all through 9th grade, had told me there was this house that the twins hung out at that was pretty cool. He was in love with Wendy and/or Katie—equally, like he couldn't decide, like a pimply wreck of a teenager like him deserved and would probably get both. They were taller than Peter and much healthier looking. They were born eight minutes apart and lived two doors down from Kim. They liked to pretend that nobody could tell them apart. Their parents partied (they called it "finding themselves") and drank relentlessly—gallons of vodka, not pints, not fifths, gallons. The girls could lift as much as they wanted. Who was going to notice? They tried to ignore Peter, but he'd discovered the lowest form of acceptance—he usually had something they wanted.

So, I followed him over one day just before the spring semester of school ended. It was Kim's house. I couldn't believe it. She still looked like Peggy Lipton. Made me feel twelve again, which was not a good thing.

A lot of things had changed in those three summers from 6th to 9th grade. Kim's mother got a job. My mother got a job. It was the mid-'70s.

Everybody's mother got a job. Her father was coming home some time that summer. They didn't quite know when. Mine had already left.

The group clicked for a while. We called ourselves the refugees, because that's what we felt like or wished we felt like. I guess that's what made us fifteen. We spelled it—"refugees"—with magnets on the refrigerator in the kitchen. We giggled a lot.

Looking back, it wasn't all that long of a time that the five of us hung out in the O'Connor's rec room. It just felt like forever.

As soon as the Major came home (to a house he'd hardly ever seen) the dynamics in the basement changed. Kim had the Major to look after. "You're responsible," her mother constantly said.

The twins claimed that he creeped them out. I don't know why, because they never ran into him. I was the one who was always running into him. So, the twins mainly stopped by to smoke whatever Peter had followed them with and then head out to the next party. Peter followed, saying he was supposed to get his license in August and that was going to change their lives, his life, somebody's lives. The O'Connor's den wasn't a refuge—it was more like a bus stop.

"What are these, man?" It was in July, hot and muggy outside and cool and muggy in the basement. Peter opened the glass cabinet that hung by the stairs on the beaverboard wall (the kind of beaverboard everybody put up in their basements) that held the Major's medals and military souvenirs. Hanging on a couple of pegs over the case was the usual Japanese ceremonial sword and sheath that every U.S. officer who'd ever been overseas seemed to have.

"They're just my dad's medals." Kim tried to push the case closed.

"What are they for? Did he get Purple Hearts and stuff?"

"I don't know," Kim said. "He never talks about them."

But see, he did talk about them—to me.

"You know what this one's for?" Mr. (he said not to call him major, because he wasn't a major anymore) O'Connor had cut off the usual route up to the kitchen. I was there alone, like usual. There was liquor on his breath, like usual. That and the smell of whatever medicine he was supposed to be taking.

"No, sir." I was standing there with a Pop-Tart from the kitchen in my hand.

"That's Korea. That's where I got my start." He rubbed his right arm. "God, I was almost as young as you." He looked at me like maybe my face would turn into somebody he knew. "This one here—the '68 Campaign, Mekong Delta. What a fuckin' mess. You know what I mean?"

"Uh-huh."

"This one's a Purple Heart. Got it going up the Hill." He expelled a breath. "We've all got our hills, right?"

"That one's kind of neat," I pointed to a shiny one.

"Good Conduct Medal. Everybody got one of those damn things." He pulled on the glass door that kind of opened like a medicine cabinet. He carefully unpinned the medal, weighed it in his palm for a second and said, "It's yours."

"Really, you sure?" I sounded like a nine-year-old kid. I wanted to ask if I could play with the sword, too.

"Can we put 'em on?" asked Wendy.

"Yeah," chimed in Katie.

"No, just leave them alone," said Kim.

"Aw, come on."

"Please."

"Just for a little bit."

Peter popped open the case, pulled a medal off the board and held it to his chest. He did a Nazi salute and said, "Hey, I'm General Pancho Villa, man, and I have given myself all these medals, man."

"What for?" squealed Wendy.

"For bravery above and beyond and beyond that, man, and for

dealing the most dope in 9th grade. And I pin this one on you." Peter pulled another one out of the cabinet and tried to pin it to Wendy's sleeveless blouse.

"Watch it, you turd." Wendy giggled and slapped Peter's hand away.

"Hey, your boobs deserve a medal as much as anybody's," Peter laughed. "How about you, Katie?"

"Yeah, like in your dreams."

"Peter, please put 'em back," Kim pleaded.

Peter pulled a couple more medals and ribbons off the board. "Hey, Danny, you need an award too, man. C'mere. I give you this, man, in the recognition of… Ouch, man, I pricked myself." Peter flicked the medal across the ping-pong table and it slid over the edge to the floor.

"Put 'em back," I said.

Peter smirked and shrugged. He reached in the cabinet once more. In the last few months he'd become a royal asshole. Some kids do that in junior high. Some do it for the rest of their lives. It was only halfway through that summer and I was praying that they would just disappear, that vacations or family reunions or anything would suck those three away from Kim and me. Peter was a good head taller than me, but I did it anyway. I slammed him against the beaverboard wall as hard as I could. The display case crashed to the floor and fell open. The medals shot out across the tiles underneath the furnace and the ping-pong table. The glass cracked.

We all froze for a second.

"Now look what you did!" Peter screamed. He tried to push back, but he was too drunk. I held him against the wall.

"Just leave, you guys. Please, just leave," Kim said. The twins had already drifted out the door and Peter slipped out of my grip and followed like a stray dog.

I was shaking like a leaf. I'd never really hit anybody before and now I wanted to do it again and again.

Kim and I crawled around on the cool floor underneath the

ping-pong table gathering up the medals. She stepped on one with a bare foot. I used a broom handle and slid one out from under one of the metal shelves. Our shoulders were touching while we stuck the medals one by one back on the board. We did it as fast as we could like that would help make it better. We hung the case back up on the wall.

"Shit, I think one's missing. I can't believe it." Kim pressed her head with her palms, wiped a tear away, mumbled, "I can't believe it," once more, and then followed the twins to a party.

The glass cabinet was there at the bottom of the stairs still hanging on the beaverboard when I went down during the funeral reception. The glass was still cracked. The missing medal—it's in a box of my stuff in a drawer in my mother's apartment.

"Move over, Stoop." Kim lay down beside me on the lumpy lopsided couch and pulled the covers over her shoulder. I'd decided to stay that night. My mother had said my father might stop by—just to chat. 'Nuf said.

"They're both up there." Kim pulled my arm around her warm waist and I spooned behind her. "I can't stand when they're both home," she said. "It's worse than when it's only one of them. They just stare like zombies. My dad doesn't say anything and my mother doesn't say anything. And I can't stand them."

I kissed the back of her neck. It smelled like nothing I'd ever smelled before. I kissed the collar of her T-shirt and the top of her ear. I kissed her hair. I wanted to kiss every strand. Kim pulled my arm around her tighter and fell asleep.

So began the summer of our gentle fumblings. It was the most wonderful and confusing time I'd ever known in my short little life. All I wanted—all I waited for was for Kim to be there. I ran, I excused myself, I left everything to go to her rec room and wait. She still went out to parties with the twins sometimes. Sometimes I went along, most of the times not. Sometimes I got stuck at home and just had to stay, which was hell. Sometimes Kim slept upstairs. She'd had a boyfriend the year before. He was like 17 or 18 or some other God-awful, unreachable thing. He'd made love to her in a car. I hated that guy with all my might. I wanted him completely and utterly erased. I did a lot of bopping of ping-pong balls.

And like life imitating art, if art imitates lies, I did end up with an early-morning paper route. My friend Ken went to camp and asked me to sub. So, I was up at five in the morning throwing papers at the screen doors of every other house in the neighborhood.

I was almost always dead tired all the time and that was almost the best part. I'd get done with the paper route around six-thirty or seven, trudge up the hill and slip through the glass sliding door of Kim's house, lay down next to her on her brother's single bed (we'd moved to the bed), and try to go back to sleep. Kim smelled warm and drowsy. I wanted something of me touching something of her all the time. Sometimes she'd get up to check on her father. Sometimes she'd smoke whatever was left from the night before. Most of the times the mornings were ours. I still love dull, warm, stupid mornings. Around ten or eleven, lawn mowers and barking dogs would start up or the phone would ring. We'd ignore all that and stay in the single bed as long as we could. I thought the month of August would be what our lives would be like forever. I thought we'd get married.

Kim's mother never seemed to be home, but there were always cookies and bologna around. So, I'd surface up to the kitchen.

"You know what I do for a living?" As usual the Major made me jump fifteen feet through the ceiling. He was always doing that. He was leaning against the doorframe to the hall and his breath smelled like an ashtray full of bourbon. He had a bottle of little orange pills in his hand.

"No, sir."

"I'm a spook. A God-damned spook."

"Like a ghost?"

"Oh, for God's sake. A spy. A spy with the C-fucking-I-A. Hell of a thing for an army officer to become."

"What do you do?" I asked.

"Used to gather intelligence, like they'd know intel if they saw it. Damn idiots. Everything they touch turns to crap. Everything."

I didn't say anything. I had no idea what to say. I was just hoping he'd go away.

"I should've seen it coming." He wobbled. "I wanna tell you something," he leaned into me. And he told me a story about the Delta, the jungle and a hill, a horrible hill, more than once, maybe five times, maybe ten. He always started at the same place and ended halfway not quite finishing what he was talking about and he always ended with what I thought was (but wasn't) halfway advice. "You don't have to take every hill. You know what I mean? Sometimes they don't even know where they're sending you. I want you to remember this. Not every hill's necessary."

I don't know why I said this, because the guy was just scary, but I kind of liked him and I wasn't scared anymore, and I just asked off the cuff, "If you don't like them, why don't you quit?"

He arched his back and pushed himself off the doorjamb. He stood up straight. He held the medicine bottle at arm's length studying it and then set it down on the counter.

"Too late for that."

"Why?" I can't believe I said that. I looked him in the eye.

He blinked and took a breath and let it expire. "Kid, you seem like a smart kid, so I'm going to give you a little bit of friendly advice."

I figured he was going to tell me to join the navy instead of the army.

He ran his fingers through his thinning too-short hair and wiped his hand over his face. "Always know where you are. Always. And if you don't know, figure it out. Figure out where you are and if you can't get out, you dig in. You understand. Don't expose yourself. You don't expose those depending on you. Right?"

I nodded. I had no idea what he was talking about.

"Don't let anybody ever tell you different. It gets so damned loud. You know what I mean? You look familiar. Do I know you?"

"I kind of hang around with Kim."

"Naw, that's not it."

I looked at my half-eaten sandwich. "Can I go now?"

"Yeah, get back to your unit."

I started to open the door to get back down to my world.

"And kid, don't you worry. We'll get you out of here. We'll get everybody out."

I read one time that the men in Vietnam liked Jimi Hendrix best. Him or Creedence. But when I was a kid all I remember hearing on the radio in those days were the Carpenters. They just owned the radio. They were on all the time. But you gotta hope it was Jimi, because you just can't quite picture guys going into battle and getting shot at and blown up singing "(They Long To Be) Close to You."

On a couple shelves in the O'Connor's rec room is Kim's brother's record collection. I guess he never came back to get them. I don't think he ever came back at all. I found myself thumbing through the collection. There was "Close to You" right next to Captain Beefheart right next to Frank Zappa next to the necessary Beatles next to the Cowsills.
"Thought I'd find you down here." Kim's voice, lower and more adult, made me jump. God, I was always jumping in that house.

I stood up. I don't think I'd ever seen her in a dress before. She was in black and in heels. I pointed to the boxes of albums. "I was just…" I said.

"Thanks for coming. It means a lot," Kim said, like she'd been saying it all afternoon, which I guess she had.

She picked up a ping-pong paddle and spun it around in her hand like she had done when she was fifteen. "You wanna keep score?" she asked, bopping the dented ball just over the net.

"Naw. Do you?"

"Naw."

We never did when we were kids.

We bopped the ball back and forth. We couldn't keep it going more than two or three times. We were awful.

On the last night that I ever saw Kim as a kid, there was an argument going on upstairs. It woke us up. It pounded us like an ocean and we were the beach. Kim's parents were having it out. I'd never heard anybody have it out before. My dad always just slammed the door and left. Kim was shivering. It was the muggiest, warmest night of the summer. We only had a sheet over us and Kim was shivering lying next to me.

"Goddammit, Fran, they're screwing with me," Kim's father screamed up above us.

I wanted to curl up into a little ball. I curled around Kim and she was already as small as she could be.

"They're screwing with everything. Me, you, everything."

I kissed a lock of Kim's hair that I'd twisted around my finger. Her shoulders were cool and so smooth. Kim tried to kiss back but her tears kept sliding between our lips. She bent her head away.

"It's got to stop. It's too loud." The Major wasn't making a whole lot of sense.

"Stop it, Jim, stop it."

Kim whispered a prayer to herself. The O'Connor's were Catholic, although I don't think they were very Catholic. I don't remember Kim doing any "Hail Marys" or nothing, but she did have a gold cross on a gold chain and it lay across her collarbone. I kissed it.

"They're supposed to be on our side," the Major screamed. "Doesn't that mean anything to them? Doesn't that mean a goddamned thing to anybody anywhere? They didn't come back."

It stormed on like that, a roar and it went on. I don't know how long.

Then it got quiet, eerie quiet. We lay there waiting for one more last shouted word or a shoe to drop or something. It didn't feel finished. But you can't keep waiting tense like that forever. I felt Kim's shoulders start to relax and her eyes start to close. I began to nod off myself. I'd catch myself and then nod again.

The door at the top of the stairs opened. The sound of footsteps came down tentatively, one at a time. Each step seemed to take longer than the last getting closer.

The light in the laundry room came on. The light in our room came on. It felt like forever, but then in one easy motion the tie-dyed sheets that made a door for the little bedroom slid apart.

"Daddy, Jesus, what are you doing down here?" Kim jumped up. She'd barely pulled on my Led Zeppelin T-shirt and her panties. I'd jumped up, too. I had a sheet wrapped halfway around my middle.

Mr. O'Connor looked around like he was running five hours, five days, five years behind everything. He ran his finger across the chipped top of the dresser like he was checking for dust. It took an eternity watching that finger. My jeans and underwear were in a pile almost shouting at him from the rug at the side of the single bed. There was nowhere to go—absolutely nowhere.

"I just thought I'd come down," the Major said.

"There's nothing going on."

He took that in. We didn't move. We leaned. We didn't look at each other. We didn't look at him.

"Where's your uniform, son?"

"Can't you sleep?" I asked.

"Sometimes, I think sleep is overrated," the Major replied.

"Do you think you need to take some more of your medicine, Daddy?" Kim asked.

"I don't think I want to take it anymore."

"Oh."

There was another long, leaning silence.

"You know, I'm sorry. I'm very sorry. I apologize. But I don't quite know where I am."

The light to the stairs clicked on. Kim's mother came halfway down and called, "Jimmie, Jimmie, come here, sweetheart. Come on, come on back up, baby."

He looked very old. He turned and slowly retreated up the stairs.

"Kim, tell your friend to go home." And the light clicked out.

I thought about staying in the woods that night, but it was drizzling outside and I fell into the creek crossing over the four boards.

I got home and my mother was up with a cup of coffee and clear, defeated eyes. She told me to sit down—that's always trouble. I sat down. I was told I was going to be going. I was told I was going to be living with my father somewhere in Michigan. It was all arranged. It was happening right away. What do you mean right away? It was happening whether I liked it or not, but it would be ok. They were really looking forward to it and I should be, too. Everything would be fine, just fine. I tried to stare hard at my mother, but I was going to cry. I started to turn my head away, but she met my eyes. She didn't turn away like she did when she told you to do the dishes. She looked me in the eye and said the most honest thing she'd ever said to me: "He's got the better lawyer."

"What about the paper route?"

"It'll all be taken care of, honey."

"But I'm responsible," I said. And what was I saying? What I wanted to say was, what about Kim? What about me and Kim and being together forever? About getting married? What about all the things I forgot to say to Kim? I'll be back. I'll never leave. I'll save you. I'll save myself. Let's keep in touch.

Kim's father's words did help. "Know where you are." I did finally find out where I was. I was in Michigan. I was there for all of high school. I ran cross-country. You just run all the time. You don't have to think. I wasn't very good at it. Sometimes I just slowed down and stopped in the middle of a race. The only thing I did right was forgive my mother. She'd found a small apartment and I went there for Thanksgivings. I tried to write a letter to Kim once, but I just balled it up.

"I used to be so jealous of you," Kim said.

I stopped bonking the ping-pong ball and just looked at her.

"You're the only one he ever really said stuff to." She paused. "I figured he must've told you some secret."

One time, maybe a week or two before I was sent away, there was a big storm. Kim's mother had hauled Kim off somewhere. Kim had rolled her eyes, but there was nothing she could do. So, I was waiting as usual. The TV was flipping. The lights flickering off and on. And I stood and watched the storm through the sliding glass doors. I liked storms. I liked the sudden coolness and the smell of warm wet asphalt.

A big clap of lightning boomed, and every detail in the basement lit up for a fraction of a second. Out of the corner of my eye there was the Major in a bathrobe and slippers in the space behind the furnace.

"Son, get away from the windows. Those are enemy rounds. Get down."

"It's just a storm," I said.

"Get down."

"It's really pretty," I said.

He darted out quicker than I thought he could, grabbed my wrist and pulled me toward his corner. I stumbled over the edge of the bed and banged and scraped my knee on the concrete floor. He dragged me the rest of the way.

"We're going to have to wait it out," he said.

"Wait what out?" I asked.

"Kid, if you're gonna survive in this man's army, you'd better get a grip."

So, we sat with our backs against a cinder block wall waiting out the storm like we were camping out or something. He had a flashlight and a compass. He offered me a cigarette and said he wished we had a few beers. I said so too, and I almost got up and looked for the half a joint in the ashtray by the bed, but then I thought that might be pushing it.

"I'm gonna tell you a secret, Davy. I'm gonna tell you something everybody better know."

"Okay," I said. "But, I'm not Davy."

"Some things are always with you. No matter what, they are always with you."

He reached into his shirt pocket. It was one of those banlon, short-sleeved shirt pockets with the little button on it and he had to wriggle his fingers in to get at what he wanted. He pulled out a small photograph, smaller than the size of a snapshot. The edges were bent. He smoothed them out.

"Here," he said. I took it and shined the flashlight on a black and white picture of his family that was maybe ten or twelve years old. I recognized him, because he had the same haircut. I pretty much recognized Mrs. O'Connor. And then there were a couple of little kids. A frowning boy, maybe eight or ten, and a little girl about three sitting on her mother's lap.

"That's what's always with me," he said.

I reached in my pocket, pulled out my thin, moneyless wallet, and handed him a postage-stamp-sized eighth-grade class picture of me. He nodded like it was a good deal. "Now, you're with me, too," he said.

The lights flickered back on. Mr. O'Connor wiped the sweat from his forehead. He opened his hand and found a couple of pills. "I guess I'm supposed to take these," he said. He went back upstairs and popped open a beer.

"He got better after a while," Kim said. "They sent him back to a VA hospital and changed his meds and stuff. They had a psychiatrist but he wouldn't talk to them. He said he'd be alright and he got okay. It took a couple of years. But he did. He went back to school and got a degree. He was like a kindergarten teacher. Can you believe that? He liked little kids. I think he was pretty happy towards the end. But he never talked about anything. I wanted him to say something so bad. I used to listen to him telling you stuff."

"You did?"

"When he'd tell you about his medals, I wanted him to tell me that so bad."

"But nothing he said ever made any sense," I said.

Kim looked around and found a couple of boxes piled with papers and old brown thermo-faxes. She pulled a few files from here and there and spread them out on the ping-pong table.

"I had to figure it out," Kim said. "I just had to. It took a long time. I used the Freedom of Information Act and everything."

She found a photo of a group of army guys leaning on a Jeep, some with guns, smiling and looking serious at the same time.

"You wanna know what really happened?"

I could only nod.

"When he was in the Army and when he was in Vietnam, he was in some kind of special-forces thing. I don't even know what the acronym means. Half the documents I got a hold of are all crossed out. They sent him in to take a hill across the border in Cambodia where they weren't supposed to be. It was supposed to be a big, big top secret and the CIA was running the operation. This is way before the bombings started. And they sent him up the wrong hill. Can you believe that? They sent him up the wrong hill. They got the coordinates backwards or some crap. Half the guys got cut to pieces and the other half got bombed by our side. And they didn't go in and get them right away, because they weren't supposed to be there."

She tapped the photo with her finger. "Everybody in this picture, except my dad, got killed. The CIA wanted to cover up"—she made those horrible quote signs with her fingers—"the 'incident.'" Kim rolled her eyes. "No kidding. It's unbelievable. So, they recruited my father.

The people who were responsible for killing everybody he knew transferred him out of the army into intelligence. Like a payoff or something. Can you believe it? It must've been so weird and he never said a word—ever."

She pointed at a figure in the photo sitting on the hood of the jeep. "You see that guy?" We looked so our heads were almost touching. A strand of her hair touched my cheek.

"Yeah, he looks kind of like…"

"Like you."

And I guess he sort of did.

"David Baufman, Private First Class. I found some old letters. My dad liked him. He looked after him." She paused, then began again. "I bet he was pretty surprised to find Davy in his basement."

She shrugged a quick half-smile, turned away and began to tidy up the pile of papers and photographs. "You know, one time my mother asked your mother for a picture of you and I couldn't figure out why. She gave it to my dad, but he said he already had one. He showed her. I don't know where he got it, but he had a picture of you."

My heart was pounding. Did he ever figure it out? Who was who? Did he have any last words?

"You ok, Stoop?" Kim touched my arm. "I guess I kind of gave you a snoot full."

I wanted it to be August again. "How'd he die?" I asked.

"Heart attack at 49. Bam—out of the blue. But I kind of like to think it had something to do with Agent Orange. I always liked a good conspiracy theory, myself." She smiled her Peggy Lipton smile.

I wanted to curl up next to Kim on that crumby musty bed. Kim said, "God, this place is a wreck down here."

"Ping pong, ping pong." A little kid came thumping down the steps one by one, toddled over to the table, grabbed one of the ping-pong paddles and banged it like a gavel. "Ping pong, ping pong."

Kim went to him. "Sweetie, stop that. Now, come on, come here, come here a minute."

"Ping pong."

"Danny, this is Jimmie." *Bang, bang.* "Jimmie, stop that. I want you to meet somebody." She picked the kid up like only a mother can pick up a kid and swung him to her hip. She beamed.

He squirmed right back down. "Ping pong."

A voice from up the stairs hollered down. "You got him?"

"Yeah," Kim hollered back up.

"Okay, because we've gotta get going pretty soon."

"We'll be right up. I'll be just a minute." She pushed some hair back from her forehead and gave a "jeez" smile. "My husband. He's stationed over at Andrews."

Behind us we heard the sliding glass door slide open and we turned as fast as we could. Kim looked caught and scared for a second. Then she relaxed. We went to the open door. We could see him fine. Her son had just left her father's den and was happily slipping and clawing up the most unnecessary hill in the world. He turned and waved, and then solemnly watched the cars go by on the highway that had finally replaced the woods.

The Old Cart Wrangler's Saga:
Cart 437 2.0: The Continuing Story Of A Man And His Shopping Cart
2016

IT'S BEEN FOUR YEARS since I chased Cart 437 across the Mart Mart parking lot, caught up with it, bought a few beers and a 12-pack of Little Debbie snack cakes—the necessary provisions—and we headed west. We planned on heading back to the Mart—eventually. We just decided on taking the long way around.

I'd been a cart wrangler for the Mart. I guess I still am, just sort of on sabbatical. I still get the employee newsletter. I do enjoy the celebrity crossword puzzles and the safety tips—wash your hands, be clean. It's the law. No problemo. Be tidy. Well, that's a good thing to be—tidy. I can be tidy. Report the suspicious—well, there's always something suspicious going on at the Mart. I'll do what I can. And be prompt—well, if it's a choice between showing up on time and getting the job done, I guess I'm going to get the job done no matter how long it takes.

I worked overtime sometimes. I gave the Mart a few of my own hours just to keep things—tidy. I liked getting all those shopping carts in a row, bashing them, rolling them, getting them lined up for the customers on the back end of another 24/7 cycle.

But you already know what happened. Cart 437 didn't line up like the other carts. Always rolled in a different direction. Turn your head for a second and it'd be around the corner, roll out of sight. One day Cart 437 broke away. Crossed the frontage road. Crossed against the light.

Just wanted to see what was on the other side. I felt the same way and here we are.

Now, unfortunately, we're being followed. The Mart Boys. You know the Mart Boys. They have badges and are trained in *security.*

We are only two days ahead of them. After all this time, only two days. The Mart Boys like to say they are Mart Men, but they're not men, they're boys. They don't know nothing of the world. They don't know how life goes on out here in the desert that is referred to on the Google Maps as the Great Parking Lot. It stretches on.

We have to lose those boys. So, we'll have to head out to the outer lot—a cross between the Badlands and long-term parking. They say not many return from out there. You can lose your sense of direction, lose your sense of hope, forget your keys, forget your kids.

It's the land of potholes out there. That'll give those boys something to think about. Holes that are a foot deep, some two-foot, some four-foot wide, some maybe a thousand feet across, ten thousand feet deep. You fall in, but you may never come back up. And who'd look for you?

Takes a while to get used to it out here. You don't just push your cart out into the unknown. Not at first. Not right away. Nobody does. You stick to the known. You stick to the curbs. You hug 'em. Met some Curb Followers once. They're a cult. They walk single file, one foot on the curb, one foot in the gutter. Up, down, up, down. The procession looks like a drunken millipede. They follow the curbs—in and around the fake lakes, the retention ponds, tracing cul-du-sacs, looping around bus stops and left-turn only lanes passed middle school afternoon pick-ups and no-standing zones like following a shoreline, like following fractals.

I have to tell you, to me the curbs are just everyday, garden-variety paths. Following the average curb will only ever lead you on a big, long higgy-jiggy cha-cha-cha rumba line right back to the Mart.

But there's a few curbs out there that don't buckle around. They simply come to an end. You stop. Maybe you turn around and go back the way you came, or maybe you shrug, you look both ways, you take one last breath and step off. That's what we did. Stepped off into parking lot incognito. Like sailing on a giant sea.

About six weeks, maybe ten weeks out from the end of the curbs we found an old abandoned strip mall that we lived in for close to two years. Lived in a Radio Shack for a while—there was plenty of room, nothing in it. Then we rolled next door to a furniture store. Could sleep on a different couch every night for a month.

Told passers-by that the strip mall was haunted just to keep 'em away. Then we found out the strip mall really was haunted. We moved on.

Ran supplies to the Clover Leaf People for a while. The Clover Leaf People are the people who live on the green median strips and in the lost spaces pinched between the interstate exit ramps and entryways. They hide behind bushes and steal hubcaps. You rarely see them. They're nocturnal. They live off of what the rush of traffic leaves behind—beer, energy drinks, and Little Debbie snack cakes (God, I love those cakes). Not a bad life.

Clover Leaf People said, come on live with them. And they are a pretty people and a solid easy-going people and my gosh, the women, oh…and I was sorely tempted; but too much mud and gravel. No good for a man and his cart. You can't hardly move. You'll end up stuck in a rut.

You need a smooth road, a smooth surface, for a cart. It's always gotta be smooth. And heaven help you if your cart throws a wheel way out here. I've thought about it. I've thought about what I'd do if this cart broke down to three, or worse even two wheels. Would I have the guts? Would I have the heart? Would I have the humility and the humanity to put the cart out of its misery?

Clover Leaf People looked over their shoulders and said, "Did you know you are being followed?" I said, Yes I did. Damn Mart Mart Storm Troopers, anyway.

I asked, Did they know they had a traitor in their midst? Looked like

I'd been sold out. They said, "Yeah, Mart Boys had bought off one of our own." What'd they get? I asked. "A coupon," they said. "A 'buy one, get one free' coupon." That was it. Betrayed for a coupon. Half price. We moved on.

And here we are. In the middle of one of the largest, most vast, most unexplored parking lots in the world. No curbs, no signs. No turning back. The Mart Boys are getting close. I can smell 'em. I can smell their aftershave.

We roll by a few abandoned shopping carts, pointed in no particular direction. Most carts show very little interest in other carts, but we watch them just to see what they'll do. Sometimes fifty or more will all of a sudden pull together in a pack and flow across the Lot like geese or wildebeest.

We pause to eye a tragic sight. There's been a standoff between two alpha carts—two bull carts. They faced off, stared and stared for days, weeks maybe. Then the two slammed together—BAM—and then slammed together again—BAM BAM and they kept on slamming—until they get stuck. Like antelope bucks with their antlers—they banged their baskets together and they got all stuck facing each other—basket on basket.

It'll rain. The other carts will move on. But the two bull carts will sit there facing each other entangled with their bent metal baskets locked together forever just staring at each other. They'll finally die of uselessness. Well, that's what we all die of, isn't it, uselessness. We move on.

A noise comes up from behind, a big hubbub. The Mart Boys are here. Sixty of 'em, maybe a hundred—all with green vests, all prematurely bald, all with ill-fitting tan pants. It's not a pretty sight, no women amongst them. If evolution had any sense the subspecies of Mart Boys would go extinct inside a week. A few are trying to pull the bull carts apart. They've gathered up a good 70-75 stray carts and lined 'em up side by side. It's going to be a flat out Napoleonic charge. They're cheating. They've brought along one of those motorized cart pusher machines with the little spinny red light on a pole.

We face the horde. For the first time I notice that Cart 437 has a chip out of one of its plastic rubber wheels. It's been limping. And it's shaking a little. I am, too. Still we stand our ground. We're about 100-150 yards away from the Mart Boy line. There's no wind, no shadows. It's noon.

A mid-management Mart Boy calls, "Alls we want is the cart. You can go, mister."

I shout back, "We're a package deal."

He says, "So be it."

And here they come pushing their carts as hard as they can. The noise, the yells, the squealing wheels is deafening. The line approaching faster and faster begins to waver and wiggle. It's hard to push a cart straight while trying to hold your tan pants up. Some of the carts bash into each other. Some roll and fall. But they keep on coming.

We stay put.

They're getting closer and closer. 75 yards. 50. Oh my, 30 yards. We don't back away. Never, never back away. And suddenly there's an ungodly shaking and screeching noise, dust and thunder. Dirt rains down upon us and the parking lot cracks open and splits asunder, you know, biblically. Splits like a pair of cheap tan pants and a thousand foot wide, thousand-foot deep pothole—ZOOM—just appears. And ZOOM. Every one of those Mart Boys and their Mart carts spill into the giant chasm like lemmings.

I wait for the dust to settle. I take a peek over the edge. Nothing to see. They're gone. Just a little puddle of water at the bottom.

It's 12:05—just after noon. The wind has died down. The hole's still there, but I imagine it'll get filled up with something. Not sure what we'll do with the rest of the day. We need a few provisions.

Wild carrots grow in the cracks in the pavement. There's always beers and snacks falling off the backs of trucks somewhere. I guess we'll keep heading into the interior, or is it the exterior, of the lot. Who knows? We're not worried. The Great Parking Lot is like a desert and like a desert it is alive. It will provide. We'll be fine—me and Cart 437.

Sewers, Dams, and Triples

1988

THAT SUMMER IT HAPPENED AGAIN. I guess I was pitching. Richard was up to bat and Tina was supposed to be catching. And it happened again. The sewer ate another ball. The ball went by the bat. We ran and the ball rolled and we ran and the ball picked up speed and we gave up. The ball didn't even hit the curb; it just went right down the hole.

"Why didn't you hit it?" I cried.

"Why didn't you throw it over the plate?"

"I did."

"You did not. It was high and outside."

"Well, you're supposed to protect the plate."

"I don't have to swing if I don't want."

Meanwhile, Tina was on her stomach with her feet out in the street and her head halfway down the storm sewer.

"Can you see it?" we asked, kneeling beside her.

"Almost."

"What do you mean, 'almost'?" Richard tried to squinch in. "Let me see if I can see."

"Can you see it?" I asked.

"Almost."

"You know, what we need is a long stick that's sort of like a pair of tweezers with a flashlight on the end of it so that you can see around corners. That's what we need."

"Yeah, that would work," said Tina. "Ick, look."

Complications set in. Mr. Ellis was washing his Ford and a thin soapy river was heading down the gutter bending around pebbles and pushing leaves towards us.

"We're gonna have to build a dam. Come on," Richard said.

I got some dirt from Mrs. Salcetti's flower bed and Richard kicked the crud and debris along the curb into a pile. We based our dam's design on the Grand Coulee—or was it the Hoover? Anyway, it started to hold water. Tina played in the puddle.

Tim O'Donnell came along. He was old enough and big enough to pry up the manhole cover, but he wasn't going to because he was with Karen. They had their tennis rackets and looked uselessly in love. I didn't think they'd bother stopping.

"Lose another one?" Tim asked with nostalgic concern.

I shrugged and Richard said, "It wasn't our fault."

Tim laughed. "Well, good luck, kids." Yeah, kids, he'd been a kid, too, until he'd grown up and gone to junior high. Then halfway down the sidewalk they stopped in a whispering huddle.

Karen giggled and pleaded, "Why not?"

Tim turned, "Here," and tossed us a scuzzed-up tennis ball.

Tina stayed with the puddle, Richard pitched, and I hit a triple over the Salcetti's car.

About a week later it happened again.

A Ford and One Pink Shoe

1987

IT WAS STILL SUMMER. It had been for a week. School was out and me and Richard knew we'd have to get serious. It was time to burn the Mustang.

The Mustang wasn't very big. It was a 1/32nd plastic scale model with a bad paint job. Richard had wanted purple and I'd wanted chartreuse, so we'd compromised on half and half with cobalt racing stripes and decal flames on the doors and hood. It deserved to die.

"We could blow it up with a firecracker," I said. "Or we could pulverize it with my sling shot."

Richard shook his head. "No way, we gotta make it look real—like a car that went flipping off a cliff."

That was true. It was going to have to look real. Like an accident. Like TV. We'd decided to be scientific about the wreck. We had the latest equipment—a BIC lighter Richard found in Billy Wilson's desk at school and to be on the safe side, I filled up a bucket of water. We were going to be methodical. First, we'd melt the front fenders and crunch them in with a stick, like the car had wrapped around a telephone pole. Then we'd light the engine on fire. Then, if the TV was right, it'd probably explode.

We knelt down behind the garage in a dirt pile. Richard flicked the lighter and the Mustang didn't quite take. The car warped and stank with thin black smoke. It looked great. Richard flicked the BIC again. A decal rolled up and melted and a small flame appeared.

"Oh no." Richard stood up and handed me the lighter and I stuffed it in my back pocket. Richard's little sister, Tina, was there with her usual Barbie in one hand and a thumb in her mouth.

"Go away," we said.

"I wanna watch," she said.

"You can't. Go away," we said.

"But I wanna burn something, too."

"You don't have anything to burn, Tina. Go away," we said.

"I've got Barbie." Tina held out the doll with its bridesmaid's dress half on and only one pink shoe.

Richard looked at me, horrified and considering at the same time.

"You can't burn Barbie," I said.

"Yes, I can. I can do whatever I want," Tina said.

"You don't really want to burn Barbie, do you?" Richard asked, reaching for the doll.

"Uh-huh."

Tina handed her brother the doll and Richard handed Barbie to me. I held the thing by its legs. Its vacant blue eyes looked right through me and I took a quick peek down the front of its dress. Couldn't see a thing.

"Ok, go ahead," Richard said.

I didn't know if he was kidding or not. Burn Barbie. I'd never thought about it. I don't know if anybody had ever thought about it, except, there had to be some kind of dirt-pile set of rules somewhere that said, "Thou shalt not burn thy best friend's sister's doll in vain."

I handed Barbie back to Tina. She took it, took a breath, and then flipped Barbie down next to the Mustang, one arm with the elbow backwards looking like it was reaching for the flames.

The Mustang was half goo and smelled like crayons in a dryer. We stood and stared. It was great, so close to looking so real. The paint bubbled up and the flames…the flames licked in Barbie's direction. Her little plastic fingers began to curl.

Richard groaned and grabbed the bucket. I kicked some dirt on the car and we salvaged what we could—one mag wheel and one pink shoe. The fire was out. Barbie was only singed. Tina sort of smiled, grabbed the doll, and, most likely, ran off to find Ken.

Under the Broken Tree Bridge

2008

ON THE WAY BACK from West Jefferson Park the creek crosses behind the ball fields, flows under the interstate, cuts a hard curve into a sandbank, and then dribbles on beyond the broken tree bridge. The highway kind of makes it like a bridge over a bridge, and it always smells dark and mummy-cold under there, but it's the fastest way home. We were on our way home.

I think Tina saw it first, but Richard says he did. We all stopped and stared at the same time.

"What is it?"

"Oh, yuck."

I swear it was a dinosaur or, at least, pretty close. It was under the fallen tree half out of the water like it had crawled and evolved as far as the sand. It had pulled-back lips and white teeth. Matted and skinny with flies. A tail where you could see the bone with bits of fur and maybe scales. And it was dead, definitely dead, probably dead, most likely.

Richard said, "It might be a million years old."

"Don't you dare touch it," Tina commanded and grabbed my hand.

We had to push through the weeds and slide down some dirt to get a closer look. Richard found a stick to poke it with and moved in. I slid down the muddy bank right behind him. We crept up to it in silence. Richard had the stick ready and poked the sand next to the carcass just a little with its tip.

"It smells like poop down here," Tina said.

Dragonflies buzzed and the sun cut under a cloud. I set my school pack down and said to Richard: "Give me the stick." Something splashed. But I didn't jump. Maybe I did.

"Did it move?"

"Naw, course not," Richard honked a scared laugh.

"Man, I thought I saw it move."

"It's definitely probably a dinosaur, but probably not a Tyrannosaurus."

"Maybe it's a raptor," said Tina.

"What do you know about raptors?"

"They've got sickle-shaped claws and they travel in packs."

"God, what are they teaching you kids in kindergarten?"

"We should call the Smithsonian."

"Or maybe the FBI."

Way off in the distance I think I heard thunder or maybe it was just the cars banging away on the bridge up above.

"Come on, help me try and pick it up," I said, and slid the stick under the creature's body until it wouldn't go any further. Richard grabbed hold and we tried to lift the fuzzy, soaked, broken-backed thing, but it just got heavier and heavier, the tail dripped, and the stick bent almost in half.

"It must be a billion years old," Tina said.

"Kinda looks like a dead squirrel."

"Naw, it's a lot more than that," Richard said in a reverent whisper. "It's much more. It's a missing link. Maybe *the* missing link. It's not mammalian, but it's proto-mammalian. This one is probably whatever came between dinosaurs and rats. Paleontologists are always looking for it. They need it."

Wow, this was big.

Then there was a crack, the stick snapped, and we scrambled over each other getting up the bank. Tina's shoes were soaked and the bottom half of my math book was wet.

"It moved. I saw it move that time."

"I wanna go home."

The ancient thing lay belly up on the shore. It had black holes for eyes and it stared at us. We thought about trying to move it again. Maybe hiding it, so nobody else would find what we found. Tina wanted to give it a funeral first which seemed like a good idea. But it was getting late, so we decided to go home, wash with soap, and come back the next day with a heavy-duty zip-lock plastic two-gallon bag, a shoebox, and a bigger stick.

The thunder was really thunder and that night it rained a hard, heavy, dark soaking rain that cleared the air and washed all the gutter trash down the storm sewers. We left ten minutes early the next morning and walked back to the broken tree bridge. We searched all around. Down the stream. Up the stream. In the cattails, but the rain must've washed away the missing link that had been searched for by so many for so long. We went on—we had to, we had no choice. We had to get to school—but I felt bad. We came so close, and science was never to recover from the loss.

The Last Deer

2011

ASH KNELT TO THE GROUND like he was a hunter or something. "Deer sign," he said, and there were marks in the mud.

"Could be a pig," I said, just to throw a wrench in the works.

"Maybe it's Bigfoot." Deana giggled.

Ash rolled his eyes, but you knew any of us would've loved to have found a little evidence of Bigfoot or the Bermuda Triangle. Who wouldn't've? We were eleven.

It was the summer of 1967 and we'd just crossed one of the many little creeks that fed Four Mile Run out of the Armed Forces Golf and Country Club up around 26th Street. It was a neat little area of no man's land where the golf course dumped brush and grass cuttings and the fence was bent low. Kid trails crisscrossed all through those woods. Every once in a while we'd cross the wooded line along the fairway and venture into the open to stuff dog shit in the 13th hole or sled in the winter, but not often.

"You think it's a buck?" I asked. I'd never hunted, but my dad was a hunter, so I knew the terms—field dressing, tree stand. We giggled at *rutting*. We always giggled at *rutting*.

"A doe, a deer, a female deer," Deana hummed.

"Gosh, you gotta hope so," said Ash. "It could be big. Wouldn't it be cool if it had a great rack?"

Deana punched him in the shoulder. "Pervert," she said. She had a lot of brothers.

"There's not supposed to be any deer in Arlington," I said, and we followed a couple more prints along the creek until they disappeared into rocks and leaves.

We lived basically in the city, on the wrong side of the river, but still inside that 10-mile by 10-mile diamond that makes up the Nation's Capital, Washington, D.C., on the map.

I think I read somewhere that the last deer to be taken legally in Arlington County, Virginia, was in 1926. My dad would've questioned that. He would've thought it was probably much earlier, maybe before the turn of the last century, maybe back as far as the Civil War. The thing is that even back in the 1940s and '50s, but definitely in the 1960s and '70s, there were a lot fewer deer around than there are today. Nowadays, deer are kind of like squirrels, but in 1967 you never saw a deer inside the Beltway.

The only time you saw a deer back then was when we drove by a beaten carcass on the side of the interstate on the way to the mountains. My dad always said, "Too bad. Could've been good eatin'."

"I wonder if it's trapped?" Deana said. She was always coming up with stuff like that. "I wonder if it can't get out of the golf course?"

We were on the edge of a bunker. A green hill rose above and away from us, and a couple golfers were maybe a hundred yards away. They waved us off. They shouted.

"We should've mooned them," Ash said a couple of hours later, a couple weeks later. Even a couple of years later he still said it with such honest regret, like if we'd mooned a couple of golfers when we were eleven years old the world would have become a better place. We did, however, leave our initials scuffed in the sand before we ran.

"I wonder if it has enough to eat?" Deana said when we were standing in front of the James Longstreet Memorial Public Branch Library where we mostly met. She fingered her rosary. I didn't know what a rosary did, but I kind of wished I had one.

Deana was from this huge, twelve-kid-or-so military family. Arlington was full of military families moving in and out what with the Pentagon and Fort Myer. Deana's family had mostly boys and only three girls. She was somewhere in the middle. They were all—I guess my mother would've said "well-mannered"—very polite, army polite. They said, "Yes, ma'am," and, "Yes, sir," to everybody and everything. I said, "hi" and "yep" most of the time.

"We going back tomorrow?" Deana asked.

"Sure, we've got to find General Lee," said Ash, because that's what he decided we should name the deer.

"What if it's a girl deer? You ever think of that?" Deana asked.

Ash shook his head.

"Then you think again."

People—adults, I guess I'm saying—would've said Deana was a pretty little thing, too bad about the blue cats-eye glasses and the slight overbite. Too bad she didn't smile more.

"How come don't you smile more?" Ash once asked.

"Because I read the newspapers," Deana said.

For a kid who was supposed to be quiet and studious, Deana had a pretty good mouth on her. I liked that. I liked her overbite. I liked everything about her, especially her stare. She could bury other kids with her stare like a cat. "If only she'd use her stare for good instead of evil," we giggled, quoting *Get Smart*. Her brown eyes matched her brown skin and reminded me of a picture I'd seen once and couldn't find again.

I don't remember quite how Deana ended up hanging out with us that summer except we were at the library and she was at the library and we were looking up things in the same books. Her house was the peeling-paint two-story rental a couple blocks away. They almost always rented to military, because military was about the only people you could rent to.

"Where you from—originally?" Ash always asked a million questions.

"All over," Deana said.

"Think you'll move again?"

"We always do."

"How come you guys don't live in Halls Hill?" Ash asked.

Deana shrugged. She didn't know that question was "politically incorrect" (a term that hadn't been invented yet) any more than Ash did. She was Black (everybody said Negro back then) and all Blacks, as far as we knew, lived in Halls Hill or Green Valley. We'd never heard of Blacks moving onto our street before, but I don't remember much being said about it.

We looked up deer at the library. The library was the only air-conditioned, free place around. You've got to remember, this was Virginia in the '60s and places like public swimming pools hadn't been invented or desegregated yet. There was just the library. We three knew more stupid, piddly facts than anybody I'd ever heard of: wingspans of World War I planes, how many babies bats have, Confederate generals, the home states of vice presidents. Deer.

"It says here deer like salt. They lick salt from saltlicks," I read.

"Or obtain it from other natural sources," Deana kept reading.

Ash went home and took a salt container from his kitchen, you know, those ones with the girl and the umbrella on it, and we went to the woods and poured it on a log. It attracted one opossum, twelve raccoons, and 50 billion squirrels, but no deer.

"I hope it's a Sika deer," Deana said because she thought they were cute, but I knew it would pretty much have to be a whitetail deer.

The rest of that summer we jumped the bent-down fence and searched the woods for deer tracks. Once we followed the paths up almost to the clubhouse where they parked the golf carts. A couple old signs leaned up against a crumbling retaining wall. They said, "Colored and white." We knew what that was about, but didn't think anybody cared anymore and wandered down the hill.

"We got time. We'll see him," Deana said. She pulled off her shoes and socks and stuck her feet in the creek. We all did.

When school started again, we didn't see Deana much, because she went off to Saint Ann's, the Catholic school, and Ash and I went back with our sack lunches and our "home-barber-kit" haircuts our mothers gave us to our final year, 6th grade, at Stonewall Jackson Elementary School.

You might have noticed by now that practically every street and school in Arlington that wasn't named after George Washington was named after something in the Civil War. Arlington was kind of like a Civil War theme park without the cool rides and water slides and had mostly bent and rusted historic markers put up by the Daughters of the Confederate States of America.

Ash took the Civil War pretty seriously, because he was named after the Civil War. He was named by his history-buff crazy father for General Turner Ashby of Lee's Army of Northern Virginia. Ashby nobly lost his life on June 6, 1862, covering Stonewall Jackson's flank during their withdrawal from the Shenandoah Valley.

I thought that was so cool. All those generals who'd crossed through this place. All Ash and I wanted to do was play Civil War.

"If you were named for a loser, don't that make you a loser?"

Ed Chapman came up with that piece of idiot logic at lunch in the cafeteria and there really wasn't much Ash could do but bring up the deer. That raised the stakes and we were called losers and liars, but we agreed to go up to the golf course and look for the deer with Ed and a couple other idiots the next Saturday.

They showed up kicking cans, screaming at each other and sword fighting with sticks. You couldn't have heard a freight train over that noise.

"What I'm gonna do is sneak up here one night with my dad's .30-06 with a sniper scope and blow that buck away." Ed held up a pump-action BB gun with a bent barrel to the "oohs" and "ahs" of his crowd. He said his BB gun shot rocks, if you got them out of the right driveway.

"You couldn't handle a .30-06 if you tried." Deana showed up.

"Could too."

"The recoil would break your shoulder."

"Would not."

"You don't even know what a recoil is." Well, she had him there. "You don't know nothing about firearms." Deana snapped the BB gun out of Ed's hands, popped it open, spilled the BBs out, and handed it back.

"It's a lot safer that way. Now get out of our woods and stay away from our deer." Deana stared. They left. They didn't say a word. They just left. I loved Deana so much then. Probably Ash did, too. How could you not? The three of us ran and skipped all the way past the library.

You know how Columbus Day turns into Halloween and Halloween turns into Thanksgiving? That's what happened. The deer just kind of melted away from my thoughts. I heard my dad say that could happen for real. He'd be hunting, look up and see a deer, and then look again and the deer would be gone.

It snowed the first of December, which was unusual for Virginia. Wet heavy flakes and school was out. My parents were at work and everybody was caught off guard. I couldn't find Ash; maybe his mother had dragged him off to another orthodontist. I pulled the sled by Deana's house and she came running out wearing one of her brother's coats and a pair of mismatched gloves. She said her mother was having another baby, so she wouldn't be missed, but she couldn't be gone for long.

Nobody was around the golf course. I was glad. There should've been a million kids up there, but there was just the wind and the usual shotgun pock-marked "no trespassing" signs. We cut over the bent fence and headed for the hill on the 13th hole.

It wasn't bad sledding. We went sitting down, but if you really want to get going on a runner sled, you've got to go down on your belly, so you can steer with your hands. Deana laid down flat on top my back hanging on and warm, and we flew down the hill, crashed into a soft drift and went back up and did it again and then again.

A couple of times later Deana rolled off, pulling me off the sled on purpose, and we went rolling and sliding to a stop. I had snow up my sleeves and down my neck. I wanted to…and she was laughing and she made me laugh.

I stood up brushing off the snow and she came over and said, "Hold still," and shook my collar and my scarf. She leaned close to me. I thought she was going to say something, but she closed her eyes and kissed my cheek. She pulled back and she stared at me, but it wasn't a hard stare. "I wish I could stay here forever," she said. "We're gonna move again. We always move. That's what the army does."

I kissed her cheek back. I couldn't think of anything to say. All I could think of was that I'd had my first kiss and it was with Deana, cats-eye Deana wearing glasses just like my mother wore, soft-lipped Deana, Black Deana, a Black girl, and I know I should've been thinking it didn't matter, and I guess, I hope it doesn't anymore, but back then in that year and in the state of Virginia—hell, any place in America—you always knew who was Black and who was white. You'd be a liar if you said different. I wondered how her lips could be so soft.

"Haah." Deana caught her breath. She put a finger to her lips and nodded over my shoulder. I slowly turned.

Coming out of the woods on the edge of the fairway was a deer. Not the biggest deer in the world, not Bambi's dad, but it had antlers and sniffed the air. It walked out into the open and sniffed at the air again. It came toward us, not really looking, and got about 25, 30 yards away. Then it looked up.

Deana had ahold of my hand. "It's so beautiful," she whispered.

The deer finally saw us and slowly bent its path back toward the woods. It slipped behind one tree and behind another, and it was gone.

"It's real. It's real. It's real, it's real, it's real," Deana kept softly saying. She put her hands together like a prayer.

"We've got to follow it. I'll get the sled," I said.

The sled was up over the rim of the knoll, a little out of sight. Deana followed.

"What are you kids doing out here?" A big fat guy with a big fat coat and a blotchy red face was standing over the sled. "Come here," he said.

The guy said it again, "Come here." And we came. I don't know why. We should've just run, but we came.

The guy looked us over and then focused on Deana. "Did you know that no niggers allowed on this golf course?"

Deana and I looked at each other blankly.

"What? I'm talking to you."

"No, sir. I didn't know that, sir," Deana said.

"You're a damn little pickaninny, aren't cha?" the guy smiled.

"No, sir, I don't think so, sir."

"You sassin' me?"

"No, sir."

"I think you are. I believe you're sassin' me. This is a U.S. Army Recreational Facility. No niggers allowed."

"But my father's in the Army."

"You got a mouth on you, don't you? Down south they hang little niggers like you." And then he turned his yellow-teeth to me. "What you doing up here with a nigger? You a nigger lover?"

I just stood there.

He waited a second. "I asked you a question."

I just stood there more. He took a step closer.

"I think you are. I believe you are a nigger lover."

I shook my head.

"You are? You ain't?"

"I… I…," I stammered. "She's not…"

"What?" He raised his voice just a little.

"No," I said.

"'No' what?" he said.

"No," I said.

"I've got half a mind to take you both down to the goddamned police. Now, 'no' what?"

"No, I'm not a nigger lover," I squeaked. My voice squeaked. I hated him.

"You better not be."

He started to step between me and Deana. I grabbed Deana by the wrist. I pulled.

I said, "I'm sorry, sir. I'm sorry. We didn't know. I'll just take her home. Okay? I'll just take her right home."

"You do that." The guy nodded and winked at me like we had something between us. It was so quick and brutal, what he said, and he made me feel like I was like him. And maybe I was. I was white. "Get out of here," he laughed and stepped out of the way.

I didn't let go of Deana's coat until we were way down the hill, around the bend, past the creek.

She pulled away from me and practically spun in a circle. "Let go. Just let go of me. Don't you ever touch me again." She shook her arm like she was trying to shake whatever was left of me off and walked ahead. We were on the gray, overgrown path that goes along the outside of the Country Club fence and empties out onto Armory Road.

We trudged, and it was trudging. We trudged past a high gate in the fence that I'd never really seen before. It looked like a gate to a football field with a rusty padlock and chain.

Deana stopped and turned. "We have to let it out," she said.

"Let what out?" I asked.

"Let the deer out," she said. Deana kicked in the snow and found a stick, an old branch, really, and swung it at the gate. Nothing happened. She swung again and it snapped.

"We've got to let it out. Find something."

"It's locked," I said, but I looked around.

"We can break it."

I pried at one of the hinges with the stick, but the stick just snapped again.

"Watch out." Deana threw a rock at the padlock, but it missed. "We have to let it out." Deana bent down and picked up half a brick and tried slapping the lock with it. She smacked over and over again until her knuckles were bloodied and the brick was in pieces. She stood back and threw what was left at the gate.

"Open up, damn you. Open up—" and Deana let out with the most amazing, most filthy row of swear words I'd ever heard.

The gate stayed shut.

"What time is it?" she asked.

I told her and Deana started to run home. I followed.

The last thing she said to me was, "Don't tell my brothers."

The next week Deana's family moved, because that's what military families in Arlington always did. Move. Send somebody to Vietnam, Okinawa, or Germany and move. I told my mother that the Black family in the rental house left.

"That's too bad, but maybe just as well," my mother said and she gave me an "it's okay" smile.

The next night it rained a freezing rain. That's what it usually did in Virginia after a hard snow—rained.

All I'd come to think about was that gate. It was near dinner and getting dark, but I got ahold of Ash and we got some supplies, a flashlight and stuff. We said we were going to walk the dog. In my house if you volunteered to walk the dog you didn't have to explain yourself. "Bye Mom, we're gonna walk the dog and rob a liquor store." "Okay, take a hat."

"What are we doing this for?" Ash asked.

"We've got to let the deer out," I said, and I had to tell him about Deana, not the kiss, just the sledding and seeing the deer and not the guy. The guy would always be my own private humiliation.

We got to the gate and broke a pruning saw on the padlock. Lost a pair of pliers in the snow. The dog sniffed and peed. We weren't getting anywhere.

"You're never going to break that lock," a voice said from behind us. He was a tall gangling guy. He had long straggly hair tucked behind his ears. He smelled of cigarettes and sweat. I guess he was a hippie. I'd never seen a hippie before. "You should just pop the hinges," he said. "You got a screwdriver?"

We handed him our bent screwdriver. He loosened a couple things on the fence, took the hammer and tapped the bottom hinge and then tapped the top hinge, shrugged almost sheepishly, and the gate fell open, twisting on the lock. He smiled.

Ash studied the guy's mustache and coat. "You look like you're out of the Civil War," he said, which was about the highest compliment he could pay.

"Well, I'm going to war, but not that one."

"What do you mean?" I asked.

"Lost my deferment. I gotta report to the army tomorrow." He didn't say it like he was talking down to us. He said it like we were his age. "Can I give you guys a little friendly advice?" We nodded. "Don't flunk chemistry. Might make a difference someday." We nodded again.

He disappeared into the sleet.

I don't remember getting back home and I don't remember why the dog didn't bark. I do remember Ash and me being soaked to the skin, and I do remember knowing the gate was open.

And even today if you drive by that corner of Club House Drive and Armory Road the gate still hangs open, hidden by vines and unmowed scrub.

Ash never understood why I stopped wanting to play Civil War. And he never understood why Deana never sent a letter. The years of junior high were silent and guarded and we rarely participated in class discussions.

Things eventually changed in the world—now Blacks can play golf pretty much anytime they want and there are deer everywhere in

Arlington—in the parks, on the Armed Forces Golf and Country Club, in back yards and down by the river.

The suburbs are full of deer. But not like our deer. Not like the one we saw—the most beautiful deer. I'm sure other people will someday spot it, maybe even Deana. But I'm also sure, I'm certain, that I'll never see it again.

A Cure for Science

2004

YOU GOT A MATCH? You got a light? Friend. You got change? You got the time? Come over here. It's all right. What's that on your wrist? Jewels? Charms? Anything in your pockets? Marbles? Lint? A line of credit? Now then—throw 'em down, leave 'em here. Put 'em in the bucket. We're gonna need 'em. Where you going? You don't have any place to be. You're with me now. Here's a cell phone with six-and-a-half anytime minutes left on it. Call your momma. Tell her you're gonna be late. You got a job. You're working for science.

We're gonna need some ingredients. A few coins. Silt. Spent shells. Fish scales. The lost and disposable—needles, bottle tops, maybe lives. Liberally add the oil from a '57 Chevy. Start a collection. Stamps. Butterflies. The pebbles from inside your shoes. Pass the plate. Pass the hat. Pass the peas. Go down to the tracks and gather the dying coals from underneath the cars left outside their worn factories. Put them all in the bucket. Throw in a few corrupt floppy discs. Take one last peek around. And don't forget to check the dumpster behind the lab. After all, this is for science.

Then, to get this started, we're gonna have to start a fire. You're gonna need combustibles, fuel, heating oil, kerosene, aerosols, maybe something from behind the couch. Add a few feathers and the dust from an ancient cedar. Wring out an old grease rag. You're gonna need a spark. Rub two sticks together. Find a Boy Scout. Make a deal. Fan the flames. This concoction's gonna get hot. It's gonna be scalding. It'll bubble. It might burst. Hotter than your palms. Hotter than two heavenly bodies grinding away in Room 102 of the Motel Super Eight on a Saturday night. This brew is gonna yearn and ache. It'll tell lies if it has to. Science often demands the most ignoble of sacrifices.

You're gonna need something with which to stir. A spoon. A crowbar. A monkey wrench. Dip it in. Find a rhythm. Start cranking that stuff. Agitate. Not too fast, not too slow. You're gonna be here for a while. Roll up your sleeves. Spit on your palms. It's gonna get loud. Gonna sound like rain, like teeth grinding, like dice rolling across a table, like bearings out of sync, like spare parts falling from the sky. It'll creak and lurch and threaten. When you can't see through the fog or breathe in the twisted smoke or feel your own contorted pounding fists. When your eyes shine with heartbroken tears. When you know there's something you missed, some kiss that could've been yours, some light you left on but you can't remember in which room. Then you'll know you've got science.

When the stuff begins to congeal and throb—the cure will be set. It'll climb out of the pot, teeter on the edge, maybe wink at you. Jump on the floor, climb up your pant leg, grab your belt. It'll repair sound, adjust your hues, congeal time, bend rules, set broken bones. Break clouds. Mend attention. Cure cancer, polio, gout, and acronyms. It'll prove all your theorems. Amend by-laws, broker concessions, and pay outstanding debts. How many bottles you gonna need? It'll change your point of view, your heart, your looks. It'll change your ways. But once it's done, you can't change your mind. We're finished here. Go home and tell your momma, ain't no cure for my science.

The Old Cart Wrangler's Saga: Cart 437 3.01: Potemkin

2018

WELL, IT'S ANOTHER MORNING ON THE LOT—the Great Parking Lot. Like the Great Lakes, like the great inland seas the parking lot has spread out across the known and most likely the unknown worlds. You might've heard of an IKEA parking lot that takes up the better part of two states. Took two months to cross it. Barren. Barren as the Badlands.

We've come over a rise, me and Cart 437. Last night we slept on a weeded median strip a couple miles outside a big box store. I can't say which box. I can't really say how big. "Sooo big," I smile and say to myself like you'd say to a little kid and bounce 'em on your knee. "How big? Soooo big."

Cart 437 has been pushing lately. Pushing hard, like it needs to get somewhere. Rolling rolling. Getting a running start downhill to roll back up the other side. Going as fast as it can. Bouncing over the cracks in the concrete.

It's been six pretty eventful, pretty okay years since I followed Cart 437 off the Mart Mart lot over a bridge, under an overpass across the highway, took a right from a left-turn only lane and followed a feeder lot behind an abandoned strip mall to the edges of the most inner of the outer lots. The winds come from every direction out there. We eyeballed it, tried to take the straightest, most direct route, unless, of course, there were distractions.

There are always distractions. And you can see them for once. You can see them, because you're walking. If you're driving you can't see a darn thing—never could. You're going too fast. But you see everything pushing a shopping cart, and to push a shopping cart you have to walk.

Once, I tried not walking. I tried to ride in the cart. But I got my butt stuck. Took three days of wriggling around to get myself out. Neither me nor the Cart have ever mentioned the incident again. I walk. She rolls.

Walking is not a bad thing. Walking solves problems, never started a problem by taking a walk. I remember I'd say to Betty, "Betty, something's bugging me. I'm agitated. I don't know what it is." And she'd say, "Why don't you take a walk around the block and see what you come up with?" I'd take a walk around the block and I'd come back and she'd ask, "Did you solve your problem?" And I say, "I can't remember what the problem was." "Problem solved," she'd say. Betty was—I don't know, everything.

Of course, we're not the only ones walking around on the Lot. There's other people, lots of other people walking around on the lot. Most of them aren't getting anywhere. They're looking for their cars. Of course, the real question is—are their cars looking for them?

Found a bank out here once, a savings and loan. I thought I'd be funny and go in and ask them if they'd change two tens for a five. Instead they gave me a loan. A trillion dollars. I said, "Isn't a trillion dollars a lot?" "Sometimes yes, sometimes no," the bank assistant manager, who looked an awful lot like the brother-in-law of Dell the Mart Mart assistant night manager, said. I asked him, "Do I have to pay it back?" He said, "Most don't." Well, it's good to have a little extra running around money.

A young woman walks by pushing a baby carriage, the old bouncing baby buggy style, black and hooded. I call out, "You looking for your car?" She calls back, "No, lost it in the divorce." I ask if there's anything I can do? She says, "No, you men have done plenty." She walks on.

There's a museum out here. The Museum of Technological and Human Indiscretions. It's housed in a 1969 Winnebago recreational vehicle, diesel with the optional canopy.

Admission is free, but Steve, Steve's the driver and curator, strongly recommends a $15 donation. "What is this, the big city?" I say. But I give him 20 bucks. Shoot, I've got a trillion of them all of a sudden, so I say, "Keep the change." Steve eyes the museum's hand-cranked antique National cash register and then stuffs the bill in his shirt pocket.

Mainly, I come to the museum to visit the permanent collection. In a locked 5-foot long dimly lit glass case there by the fire extinguisher is the longest pubic hair known to man. 14 foot 6 inches long. It folds back and forth three times. I can't help but stare. I just can't help it. You'd say you wouldn't but you would…fourteen foot six inches long…

They've got the usual giant ball of string. Every decent museum's got one. Reputed to be the world's twentieth largest. Not bad for a Winnebago. The largest giant ball of string, of course, is owned by a Russian oligarch who moved it to Minsk. Apparently, Minsk needs string.

Finally, in the Firearms and Appliance wing there's a mint condition 1947 Whirlpool wringer washer machine that took five blasts from a 12-gauge shotgun and never missed a rinse cycle. That's American ingenuity at its best. I should tell Steve his shorts are still in there.

Instead, Steve says, "Storm's coming."

I wander back out into the sunlight or what's left of it, lean on Cart 437, and she starts to roll. The light isn't exactly light out here anymore. It's defused. There is a storm coming. A plastic storm. Plastic jugs and plastic bags float on the wind like ghosts. The stuff collects and clings and sometimes you just have to wade into a wave of the stuff, hip high, shoulder high. The plastic washes around you, like the tides. There are places on the Lot where the plastic has accumulated deep enough and thick enough that it affects the moon.

I hear a baby crying. The plastic is swirling and crackling and popping (of course it's popping, the popping sound is the sound of bubble wrap popping), but there's definitely a baby crying above the din.

"You again," the young woman says. And I say, "Hop on." And she says, "I don't need your help." And I say, "Your little baby buggy can't take the wind. I'm set up for it. I've got sails. I've got a big sheet of plastic. You've got to fight plastic with plastic, you know. Then we'll run with the storm." I mention that we've got ballast, but I don't mention that our ballast is a case of beer and a trillion dollars.

The plastic wind shakes the ground and the woman says, "Oh, what the hell," and she hands me the baby and we struggle, as one always does with a baby, to get its little legs tucked into the fold-up metal shopping cart baby seat.

The young woman smiles like she wants to be reassured. She lets go and she's gone. She's taken by the wind and at the same moment our sails are filled. Cart 437 cocks around and takes off faster than I've ever seen her roll.

We've sailed for ten days. We spun like Dorothy. We avoided whales wherever possible. And I swear we bumped down a long and wide flight of stairs.

Finally the winds died down and we've been deposited on the edge of a shallow rippling pool of water. A couple of ducks quack by—quacking that it's their puddle. There's a big box store over there. Looks familiar. It is familiar. It's the Mart. My Mart. We've come full circle after all this time. The little baby giggles.

We aim for the entrance. Can't help it. We're swept toward it. Everybody's headed for the entrance—pushing carts, pushing carriages, riding electric scooters. We're all going for the same door. Must be a sale on or maybe it's just Saturday. I can feel the cart wrangler in me keeping an eye out for strays.

"About time," the baby's mother says. She's leaning on a beat-to-hell 1984 Ford F-150 pickup truck.

"Trade in your baby buggy?" I ask.

"Renegotiated the divorce settlement," she says. And suddenly she wells up in tears. "Oh thank you, thank you for saving my baby."

And I say, "It's nothing. It's what we do. It's what a wrangler and his cart are made for. Can't help but help."

"I got to get to work," she says and she grabs her baby, the baby bag, the baby bottle, the fold-up baby stroller, the baby snacks, and the big stuffed baby bear. I didn't even know she'd stuffed all that stuff in Cart 437. She digs down one last time, grabs a beer and accidentally grabs a good portion of the trillion dollars. They hop in the truck and they're gone.

She can have the trillion. I probably should've said something though, told her what happens when you get a trillion dollars. Not pretty. When you have a trillion dollars you have to hang out with other people who have a trillion dollars. Gives me the willies just thinking about it.

Marge the greeter, who doesn't look a day over 90, bless her heart, is walking, practically marching out the front door. I catch her marching by and I say, "Where you marching off to, Marge? It's not break time yet."

She flicks her Marlboro down on the ground, stomps it out and says, "Don't you know, they're laying off all the Greeters. They're going to replace us with robots."

"That's a bummer, Marge," I say. "What're you going to do about it?"

She says, "We're going to organize. We're going to start a Million Greeter March."

I'm not much of a joiner myself, but I say, "More power to you, Marge. How many Greeters do you have signed up?"

She says, "Well, so far there's me, Ed, and Barrett."

I say, "Well, make sure Barrett's got a few Snickers and his oxygen tank and he'll be fine. Didn't you meet old Joe Mart, the original Mart Mart Man, one time?" I ask.

"Yeah, I did," Marge says. "He said I'd always have a place here. I shoulda pissed in his gas tank when I had the chance."

Words to live by, Marge, words to live by.

I push a couple carts back into their rows and I pull another one to the side out of the way of the foot traffic. Can't help myself. Got to tidy up.

"You coming?" I say over my shoulder. I've seen that Cart 437 is already dreaming of being a silhouette on a little ridge face west toward Easton a quarter mile out.

We'll go in, but just for a minute, just for provisions—Little Debbies and beer. Then it's back outside. I can't stay in there. I'm a cart wrangler and that's my calling—to follow my cart wherever she goes.

We'll go down aisle nine. We'll slip out through the emergency-only loading dock door and then we'll circumnavigate the Great Parking Lot once more.

The latest research says the Great Parking Lot is like the universe and like the universe it is forever expanding. That may be, but my feeling is that infinity doesn't go nearly as far as it used to. We'll see about that. We'll see what's in a few more of the scratchy corners of the world, and we'll see you down the road—me and Cart 437.

A Fist Full of Keys

1988

I've got a fist full of keys and I'm making noise like a janitor in a quiet hall. Keys give purpose and a little bit of credibility—there's got to be a door, right? Here's one to my front door and this one's to a deadbolt. This one's to the trunk of a Subaru I sold a couple of years ago. And this key I simply found. Sometimes I try this foundling on parked cars or empty apartments or I even try winding clocks. I could get lucky.

I keep my keys, all on a chain along with the rabbit's foot and the hangnail clipper. I've got keys from all the houses I've ever lived in, even a couple of motels (Rm. 10—Please deposit in any U.S. Mailbox—Postage Guaranteed). I still have my first key, though the lock was stolen and the bike is long gone. When I was ten I found my first skeleton on the floor of Grandma's garage in all its mysterious uselessness and rust. I held it in a tight fist in my pocket—double protection. I asked if I could have it and Grandma gave me two more. The age of encouragement.

Nine out of ten keys outlast their locks. Forgotten, they move from drawer to drawer or hibernate among string and twist-ties to brood and remember. Others seek hope and solace in the terrible and the moist. It's quaint, but look under your doormat.

Keys are only perfect—or useless. That is so like the powerful. Either doors open easily or not at all. But I don't keep keys for their niches. I keep them for their chances. In my pocket are a few dozen possibilities that I might be let in where others may only knock and then turn and walk away. Of course, if I were truly worried about getting in, I would have collected doors.

Dog Toys in Space

2009

Nicco the dog
Has a squeaky toy.
Well actually,
He has a lot of them.
We keep buying them.
He keeps, um, well—misplacing them:
    A rubber dog bone under the couch,
    An official Pizza Hut frisbee platter
        In the neighbor's hedge,
    A stuffed doe-eyed Hello Kitty
        Out by the highway.

Nicco
Prides himself on how well
He hides his toys.
Out at the Mauna Kea Observatory
They've been counting and recounting
The number of satellites
In our solar system.
    They've logged a new one.
    They're not sure. It's small,
    But it appears to be a red rubber
        Squeaky fire hydrant
    Floating around Jupiter.

The New Renaissance

1989

I'm getting ready for the new Renaissance. I've got the pointed shoes and I've been to the inquisition. I'm preparing for the new Renaissance. I'm painting the ceiling and studying anatomy. I'm getting ready for the new Renaissance. This time it will be held on the far and contemplative side of Venus.

I'm serious about this new Renaissance. I've taken an interest in physics—a screw is an inclined plane. In medicine—the heart is a lonely pump. And of course, in geology—there is a rock in my shoe and it is over a billion years old. There will be a place for logic in the new Renaissance—industry is alchemy, as alchemy is art, and art is behavior, and behavior is chance, and chance is rhythm, and rhythm is revolution, and revolution is measure, and measure is concern, and concern is aware, and aware is self, and self is gratification and, well, as this syllogism so eloquently proves—industry is masturbation. Or is it the other way around?

When the new Renaissance arrives, we'll all join committees to decide where to put the monuments. There'll be music and hymns and calculations. Four-part harmonies will be performed by trios. The scales of justice will be apprenticed and balanced by the theatre. We'll predict the outcome of cataclysms and annotate our observations with secret left-handed script. We'll march off to Italian restaurants and order things not on the menu. We'll cook and eat each other's inventions. We'll be well-read and serve no one master. When the Renaissance arrives, we'll name our firstborn "Leonardo."

During the new Renaissance, we'll stand in the ashes of assassinations and impose order on rust. We'll walk up the steps past the columns through the glass and iron doors and kiss the marble in an attempt to satisfy that awful and most ancient of civilization's gods—debt. We'll leave a tip. We'll cease to consume and truly learn. We'll conserve. We'll argue over the nature of traffic. How could those of the late Dark Ages have spent so much time waiting to go in one direction, when the machines of the new Renaissance will go backwards, forwards, sideways, and upside-down all at once?

The Tiniest Souls

2007

ONCE WE WALKED ACROSS RAZORS like they were bridges. Once there was a drought and we crossed the last puddles in a leaf. Once…

We were bigger for a while, once. Maybe sixty, seventy years ago we were the Little People and we visited Daniel. We found him when he was three. Then, we were tall, about half his height. We hid in the bushes behind the garage and drove his toy trucks. We lit fires and sang. We didn't like the brat across the street and put bees in his shoes. We sacrificed a squirrel and buried it under the porch.

We took to Daniel and like crows we liked the shiny, useless things that surround so many people. We made off with wind-up toys, loose screws, bolts and string, wallet-sized school pictures, cat whiskers, and those little mustard packets from Dairy Queen. I loved mustard. Daniel knew when we slipped into his kitchen, slamming cupboards and spilling milk, we were really looking for his mother's jewelry and his father's watch. He knew he couldn't give up those treasures, so he gave us what he could—triple A batteries, M&Ms, and his sister's Barbie's barrettes.

We kept everything we found in one pile. We watched that pile closely to see if anything would spontaneously combust or congeal. We were the descendants of alchemists.

Only Becca told Daniel her name and I can't help but think that was a mistake. We left leaf-like smudges on his windowsill and often went on sojourns for months, sometimes years. Whenever we came back we were fewer and smaller.

We were about Barbie doll sized in the years when we'd find Daniel lying on his stomach on the floor of his room on afternoons after school. The sun filtered in, warm and lazy, and we would spit on his homework and move decimal points in his equations. We were not fans of commas or semicolons and we rewrote the endings of the duller stories he was assigned. We slept in his shoes and used his pencils for stilts. We were appalled at his education and always would be. We were puzzled by the big people's misunderstanding of geography. They only drew crude maps of lands that were large and didn't seem to know, like everything, the real world doesn't get bigger it only gets more and more minute and spirals inward—places inside places inside places. Inward is where the universe goes.

We walked among the patterns of autumn frosts and crossed the thinnest ice.

Becca lingered and stayed behind sometimes by herself. Daniel was coming of age and she'd dance and pace barefoot across his skin until he was dizzy. Her kisses were breezes and her touches were whispers. They whispered together.

"Are you fairies?" he'd ask, because she was the size of a small fairy. And she'd shrug and shake her head. "No wings," she'd say.

"You're real, aren't you? And why are you so small? Why are you getting smaller? Why aren't you growing like me?" He grew sad like boys sometimes do. Becca drank one of his tears.

In the decades to come we left Daniel and walked across the last razor's edge and entered the wilderness. Middle age takes forever and goes by so quick.

A few of us heard that Daniel has three grandchildren. He accidentally called them Becca. He showed them how to catch snowflakes with your tongue. He tasted one that landed on the back of his hand. It tasted like a tear. He drank us.

At that point we were the size of pinpricks. Now we walk through the walls of his cells and joy-ride his viruses. We unbraid his dreams and swim in his veins.

We are the tiniest of souls and we have crossed and recrossed the vast emptiness between his neuropeptides and ionized particles. It's so far that we have to rest. We've found an abandoned campsite in his forgotten memories. It's a sheltered place and there's a nice view. Daniel's thoughts are like a wind and Becca lets it blow through her hair.

We are the tiniest of souls and Daniel thinks that we have killed him. But that's not true. He is the universe and he is our home.

The End of the Bike Trail

2019

THE BOAT ROCKED OVER THE EASY RIPPLES.

"I can't believe it. Missed again."

I threw another rock and Drew threw another rock at our watermelon boat floating past us on Four Mile Run.

Finally I made a splash just a few inches—well, maybe a foot—from the boat and it spun and rocked and got caught on a broken branch floating in the shallows.

"Now we got it," Drew said. He threw a medium rock and it knocked off one of the popsicle stick oars. "Oh yeah, destruction."

Drew and I jumped up and down like the little kids we weren't supposed to be anymore.

It was the beginning of summer. We were thirteen going on fourteen and there was absolutely nothing to do, so we went up to the end of the bike trail, which is what we always did.

We had six sticky quarter wedges of watermelon rinds that we'd gotten out of the trash from Drew's sister's ninth birthday party, and we'd stabbed sticks for masts and popsicle sticks for oars into the rinds to make them look like ships. They were masterpieces of impermanent folk art with catalpa leaves for sails, acorns for barrels, and twigs for cannons. We pushed them one at a time out into Four Mile Run and then threw rocks at them until they sank.

We used to do it with beer cans, but there's something about hitting a watermelon with a rock that can't be beat. Except this time we kept missing.

"Crap, what's the deal?" I tried an underhand toss and still missed by three feet.

Then, *blam!* The watermelon boat blew up into a half dozen pieces and popped a foot out of the water. Direct hit with a baseball-sized creek bottom rock.

"Hey, Donny," Drew called across the creek.

"Hey, you idiots. Whatcha doing?"

"Nothing."

"Looks like nothing."

"Well, it is nothing." Drew and Donny said this to each other every time they saw each other. They'd known each other since kindergarten. I was the junior high newcomer.

"Float another one of those suckers out there. I wanna see if I can do it again."

"Ah, come on," I said. "You can't have all the fun."

"Sure I can."

Drew ran and got our second to last watermelon ship and pushed it out into the middle of the creek. Donny chucked another rock and it just missed.

"Now you got me pissed off," Donny said, smiling. He was bigger than us, taller than us. He hadn't been that way for long, maybe six months. He'd just shot up. That's what his mother told Drew's mother anyway. He was a year or so older than us and his voice was an octave lower suddenly and he had a hint of a mustache and some stubble on his chin. He was wearing a "Bud's Motor Ways and Repairs" gimme hat, because he worked there fixing lawnmowers. His hair was sandy, shoulder-length, and tucked behind his ears. He looked so cool. Couldn't tell him that though.

"All right, all right," I said. "I'll count to three and we'll all throw at the same time."

"One, two, three," Drew said as fast as he could and we all threw.

The watermelon boat exploded into a million watermelon pieces. We'd all hit it at the same time. The only things left floating were a couple of popsicle sticks.

"Yes, yes, destruction," Drew shouted, pumping his fists and we all jumped up and down like little kids.

"I'll get the last one," I said and I ran and got the last one. It was the best one. It had a toy army man holding a bazooka standing on it. "You ready?" I said, and I gave the watermelon rind a good push to get it out past the sandbar and into the slow current.

Drew picked up a really big softball-sized rock and said, "Okay, here it goes." But he waited. "What?" he said to Donny.

Donny had his arms folded. He shrugged. "Let it go," he said.

The watermelon boat spun a little, sped up, and rode over a little rapids. It stayed upright just barely and then caught the current, spun, and in a minute or so had disappeared into the shadows under the railroad trestle.

After the first ones, the next ones don't hurt as much.

That should be the motto written on a plaque hanging outside the vice principal's office in our old junior high.

I ducked and another one went flying by, and then another, and then another one fell apart in the air. It rained down in the bushes and some of it went down the back of my shirt. I stood up and took a wild throw that curved off and landed in the creek. Somebody laughed.

We were in the middle of a dirt clod war. I don't know if dirt clod wars actually get declared, but we were fighting some kids from north of Lee Highway. We didn't even know their names.

Drew, little Jimmy Reynolds, Donny Bowers, and I had gone up to the end of the bike trail where Arlington petered out and East Falls Church began. There was a huge orange pile of dirt up there, a giant hillside of Virginia clay that was crisscrossed with mini bike paths and

BMX jumps. Over the summer we—mostly Drew and Jimmy—had dug a trench about twelve feet long and started a cave that looked down over the creek. It was a pretty good start of a fort and we needed it. We were being bombarded.

The nine north-of-Lee-Highway kids (that's a lot of kids) were on the other side of Four Mile Run. They didn't have as much dirt, but they had the whole sand bar to run up and down and they had low reeds and bushes to duck behind. They were spread out.

"Don't let them cross the creek," Jimmy shouted. "We can't let them outflank us." Jimmy always wanted to be a general.

But he was right. If those kids crossed Four Mile Run they might be able to cut into the woods and get up behind us.

A couple of them, the younger ones, had taken off their shoes and were wading. Donny tossed a big clump of clay and it splashed in front of them and it soaked them. They laughed and started slapping water and splashing themselves. The little waves rocked what was left of one of our watermelon boats.

Another clod exploded just above and behind us, and then another. We all ducked back down into our ditch.

"Incoming," Jimmy called.

"You're supposed to say incoming before they come in, you doofus," Drew said, wiping dirt off his shoulder.

"We need a shield," Donny said.

"We've got this," I said. It was a long piece of grimy cardboard from the giant box my mother's washer had come in that we were kneeling on. It was kind of comfy. It helped your knees a lot.

"Not stiff enough," Donny said.

Drew stood up with an armload of five or six clods and chucked them rapid-fire. "Hey, I hit one," he screamed. "I hit one." And he jumped back down.

It got quiet for a second or two. It kept quiet. We could hear the two kids who'd kept splashing, but nothing else.

"What's going on?" Jimmy said. "Did we win?"

It kept quiet for a little bit more.

A heavy thump hit and sprayed dirt in front of us. The dirt got in my teeth. Another hard thump hit the clay behind us. Then it sounded like gravel raining down on us. Gravel?

Jimmy stood up. He was peering out, and shading his eyes with his arm. He got hit. He slid down going, "Ow, ow, what was that?" He had an immediate red and nasty welt on his forearm the size of a plum or maybe a baseball.

"What the hell?" Donny said.

"That was a rock," Drew said, picking it up at his feet. It was about the size of something between a golf ball and a small peach.

Another rock came, and then four more. We all had our backs to the outside wall of our trench, covering our heads.

Donny took a breath and stood up, "Hey, what the hell? Just dirt clods, man. No rocks. What's wrong with you?" A rock thrown pretty hard went whizzing by his head. Donny kept standing and spit.

"All's fair, mofo," a blondish guy with Beach Boys kind of hair hanging in his eyes and braces on his teeth shouted. He was standing a little closer than the rest. One of the guys behind was trying to lob some rocks over our wall.

"We're going to die," Jimmy slumped.

"You're gonna kill somebody," Donny shouted over his shoulder

"So what?"

"We don't have any rocks," I shouted. I peeked out and a golf ball sized rock hit me in the shoulder.

"You do now."

A few dozen more baseball-sized rocks came banging in and around us. Some of the kids were standing ankle-deep in the creek, picking up ammunition and laughing their heads off.

"We need some rocks," Jimmy said, rubbing his arm.

Drew looked around. "They're crossing," he said. "They're crossing and they're coming up here."

"That's okay," Donny said. "I've got a plan."

He drew the plan in the dirt.

A few more rocks backed with a few laughs came banging in.

Jimmy's welt had turned into a cut and my shoulder ached. We had to do something.

"Roll down your shirt sleeves and put on your coats," Donny told us. It had gotten pretty hot out, but we put on our coats. "Turn up the collars," Donny said. We turned up our collars. "You know what to do?"

We nodded like we knew what to do.

"Put as many rocks in your pockets as you can. Small rocks, not big ones. Just make sure you can run."

I pulled out a big one, left it and stuffed in two smaller ones. Drew and I grabbed the piece of cardboard. Three of us got behind it, Jimmy in the middle, and moved out around the left side of the trench.

"And don't stop. Don't stop for anything," Donny called before he disappeared over to the right end of our trench.

We did what we were told. We stepped right out into the open. Me, Drew, and Jimmy got pelted with rocks. The cardboard buckled and blocked a lot of them, but my thighs and ankles were dying. The kids were moving toward us, climbing and sliding up the dirt hill.

We didn't have many rocks left and me and Drew could only use one hand apiece, because we were trying to hold up the cardboard, but we did have Donny. We always had Donny. They didn't see Donny. Donny whooped around from the other end of the trench like he was in a war, like he was in a movie, like he was going to save us, and we believed he would. We cheered, because what those Lee Highway kids didn't know about Donny was that if he wouldn't have been suspended for smoking a joint in the parking lot with some kids who weren't even from our school (I mean really, what a cliché) he would've been first-string shortstop for the Knights of Columbus Babe Ruth League team. He was that good. He could throw anybody out from any position moving to his right or his left, from his knees, side-armed, it didn't matter. If he got the ball, the ball was going to first base fast and accurate.

And that's what he did to the north of Lee Highway boys. Ran them down and threw them out. They stumbled and splashed and fell trying to cross back across the creek. The blond guy tripped to his knees and was soaked to the waist. One kid was crying. He had a cut on the side of his cheek. Another said he lost his glasses. It was a battle. It was a rout. It was like the Civil War.

We turned and ran, headed for home.

"See you guys later," Donny called running past us down the bike trail.

"Boys are such idiots," Lizza said.

"Yeah, we are," Donny said, smiling the stupidest smile I've ever seen in my life, holding Lizza's hand with one hand and eating fries with the other. I'd run into them at the Putt Putt. I'd never hung out with them before. It was like being let into a place I never even knew existed.

"Isn't Lizza with an 's' and not two 'z's," I asked, looking at the bracelet that Donny had given her.

"It can be either way."

"Isn't it usually with an 's'?" I asked.

"Well, I changed it."

"You're allowed to change the spelling of your name? I didn't think that was allowed."

"Yeah, you can change the spelling of your name. You can change your name. I think everybody should be able to change their names. As a matter of fact I don't think kids should have names, I mean permanent names, until they are like ten or twelve. Then I think everybody should be allowed to name themselves." Lizza acted like this was a major legal question. "I think minors should be emancipated," she said.

"She thinks everybody should be emancipated," Donny said.

"Except you," Lizza smiled. "I own you." They kissed.

"Yeah, you do."

We were sitting at one of those orange plastic tables with the attached orange plastic benches on the other side of the paint peeling orange fence from the 18th hole at Putt Putt. The table was hot and the bench was hot to the touch because the sun was so hot. It was July in Virginia.

We had been trying to explain the dirt clod battle to Lizza. I was doing most of the talking, because I was excited and talking too much and Donny was the hero of the story, so he couldn't really tell it because it would be like bragging.

"So, you were throwing rocks at each other?"

"Well no, at first it was just dirt," I explained for the second or third time.

"Yeah right, dirt. Where was this?"

"At the end of the bike trail," Donny said, like everybody knew where it was.

"You mean up there past Roosevelt?"

"Yeah."

"Gross, gross, gross. I haven't been up there since I was a little kid, like twelve. It's like a radioactive nuclear waste dump up there."

"It's not that bad." Donny sounded offended.

"No, it's cool," I said. "Like a park, our own private park. We camp up there and everything."

"Used to camp," Donny corrected.

"No, we still are. Me and Drew. We were talking about maybe doing it next week. Build a fire. Get some marshmallows and maybe beer. You guys oughta come. You could have your own tent and stuff."

"Naw, she'd be afraid of the bears," Donny winked at me.

"Bears? There are bears up there? Bears in Arlington County?"

"Not many," I said. "Maybe just one. One big one."

"I'd protect you," Donny said gravely.

"You would, would you? What would I have to do? You know, to get protected?" Lizza leaned in on Donny. She almost looked like a boy, like the most beautiful boy in the world. She said she'd cut her hair a couple weeks before. She'd cut it really short. Almost all the other girls had long, long hair, long Peggy Lipton hair sometimes way past their waists. Lizza looked like an elf, the most gorgeous elf in the world.

"You wouldn't have to do much," Donny started laughing.

"I know what I might have to do," Lizza said. "I might have to tickle that bear."

"Oh no, come on, Leez, no…" Donny and Lizza started hand slapping. Then Donny hopped up, rounded the table, and grabbed his Dr. Pepper. "Don't come near me. You'll get wet, I swear."

"Did you know that Donny's ticklish? It's like his kryptonite." Lizza stalked toward Donny wiggling her fingers. "Come on, I won't hurt you."

Donny was doubled over laughing. "Stay away," he said.

"Nothing I can do, Donny," I shrugged.

A car honked behind us. We didn't pay any attention at first. But the honk wasn't a friendly honk. I'm not sure how you can tell, but it wasn't.

The guy in the car had rolled down the passenger side window and was leaning over and saying something. Then he shouted it. We walked closer. We couldn't understand him.

"Meow," the guy said. I knew him now. He was the Beach Boy hair guy from the dirt clod war.

"What?" I said.

"Meow, pussies," he grinned.

"Why's he talking about cats?" I said.

"You've got to be kidding," Lizza said.

"That's really stupid," Donny said.

"What'd you say?"

"I said…that's…really…really…stu…pid," Donny said really slowly and acted like he was making sign language.

"You wanna do it? You wanna do it right here?"

I started to back up. I didn't like it. But Lizza leaned in the passenger side window. "This your mother's car?" she asked like she was serious. "You should get one of those little pine tree air fresheners for it." She noticed a little five-year-old sister sitting in the back seat. "Hi, sweetie," Lizza said.

"Get the fuck away from my family," Beach Boy said.

The Ford Torino station wagon squealed its wheels or tried to squeal its wheels and took off.

"Definitely his mother's car," I said.

"Guess he doesn't want to play putt-putt," Donny said.

"Prep school kids. Frickin' assholes," Lizza said. "I hate 'em."

"How'd you know he's prep school?" I didn't really know what a prep school was.

"He had his uniform on," Lizza said. "Little rich shits. I hate Stafford Prep."

"Why do you hate them so much?" I asked. I'd never heard Lizza talk that way. Well, I didn't know how she talked. I didn't know her that well. She was already in high school, but she was spitting mad, spitting hate.

"My sister dated one one time. They are dicks. Little rich dicks," she said. "They think they can do anything, buy anything, take anything they want."

Donny hung an arm over Lizza's shoulder. "You wanna play another putt-putt? I'll spot you ten points. I'll play left-handed."

"I'll play," I said, because, well, it was putt-putt and usually my mother only dropped me off with enough money for one round. Then I thought, "I didn't know there were rich kids in Arlington. I thought we were all the same."

"Naw, there's them and there's us," Donny said.

"They're rich snots and we're blue-collar," Lizza explained.

"She means white trash."

"We're white trash?" I said.

"No," Lizza said. "You live over by Bon Air. That's the middle, middle class. Don't worry about it."

"Maybe I oughta get a little coat and tie," Donny smirked. "I'd make a good preppie."

"Somebody oughta sue their asses," Lizza said.

"She's gonna be a lawyer," Donny said.

"Really?"

"Yeah, I am."

"So, what do you think that guy was doing over here?"

"Robbing from the poor and giving to the rich," Donny said.

"What sucks is they don't just take what they want, they take what other people really need, and we're so dumb that we let them. Read Engels. Read Thorstein Veblen."

"Well, I've got all that I need," Donny said.

"What?"

"I've got you," he said to Lizza, pulling her close and kissing the top of her head.

"You're so stupid," she said, and she leaned closer.

"We could still go camping," I said.

"Yeah, maybe we oughta go camping," Donny said.

"Maybe," Lizza said.

"Ah, no," I said. "I forgot. I've got to go to my Grandma's."

"You'd rather hang out with your Grandma than us?" Lizza acted all hurt.

"Well, it's not my choice. It's not my fault," I sputtered.

Lizza laughed. "Don't worry about it. Who is this kid? You are such a sucker."

The Ford Torino station wagon came back through, coming out of Hecht's parking lot honking and flipping us the bird.

Donny Bowers was dead before the end of summer.

I was at my Grandmother's past the end of summer, way past fall.

My parents had had another fight, another separation, another list of ultimatums. They argued about where I should go. My father wanted me in Houston where he was going, but he was traveling and wasn't going to be there yet. My mother wanted me back at the house, but she was selling the house and she needed time. So, I was left at my Grandma's. I didn't mind so much.

In the spring I ended up back living with my mother in an apartment north of Kirkwood Drive. She'd petitioned to get me into an arts magnet school. I was on a waiting list for a while. Then I went. I didn't know anybody.

I can't remember how I found out Donny Bowers was dead. He'd been killed about two weeks after we'd played putt-putt. He'd been beaten to death. He'd been beaten to death at the end of the bike trail.

Nobody said anything, not six months later. I don't remember any mention from my mother, or community discussions or school board memorials or plaques in the halls or any newspaper op-eds about "kids these days." There were no flowers left on the side of the road. There must've been a funeral. I guess I missed the funeral. I guess I didn't really know Donny well enough to be invited to his funeral. I'd never been to a funeral.

Donny was beaten into a coma. He never woke up. They used sticks and rocks. They kept on hitting him. Some rumors said that there were also baseball bats and crowbars and pipes. Sometimes there were nine of them, sometimes twelve, sometimes fifteen. It was maybe a gang from D.C. It was maybe the Hells Angels. But it was kids—kids between the ages of thirteen and seventeen. They used sticks and rocks.

I don't remember a big trial. I don't remember a trial at all. Three "youths" were charged with assault and were released into the custody of their parents by the juvenile court. The youths were tried as minors and the records were sealed. It was noted that the youths were from good families and I can only imagine that they graduated with honors and went on to law school, maybe the Supreme Court.

There were other youths involved—kids that saw, witnesses. Those youths were probably Jimmy and Drew, but I never saw their names listed or found out for sure. I never saw them again. We'd always just met in the park, because that's what we did, and going back to the park and waiting for them didn't seem like it would do any good.

I don't know why I hang on to this story, because it just keeps looping around and going nowhere. The murder wasn't a prototype for Parkland or Columbine or Bennie and the Jets. It wasn't proof of anything. It just was. It happens all the time. It can happen anywhere. The murder was treated like an accident. You could almost hear parents telling their kids to turn away and not to stare.

Once I tried walking up to the end of the bike trail, but I stopped. I couldn't go any further. I didn't want to sink any more watermelon boats. Darkness had arrived. I'd never known darkness before, but now I knew where it was and what it did. Darkness flew over me and blocked out all the light just for a second, for a minute. It flew over Donny and blocked out the light forever—forever and on purpose.

There was a day, a single day, when I wanted to be Donny, that putt-putt day, that one day when I hung out with Donny and Lizza, I wanted to be Donny. I wanted to be kissed by a girl who looked at you like nobody had ever looked at you before. I hang on to that even though it's not mine. It's not mine to keep, and still I keep it.

I think I saw Lizza one time a few years later. She was lifting a kid out of the back seat of a car. Her hair was still short.

I found this 1973 Northern Virginia Ledger clipping in my mother's top dresser drawer after her funeral. She'd kept it. She'd kept everything and never said a word:

> YOUTH DIES IN BEATING – A 16-year-old youth died in County Memorial Hospital Thursday of injuries he suffered when he was severely beaten by nine youths last Friday at the end of county bike trail. Donald Bowers lost

consciousness shortly after he was admitted to the hospital about 9 p.m. and was in a coma until his death, officials said. Authorities said the youth was repeatedly struck about the head, chest, and stomach areas with rocks and sticks and was kicked. All the youths between the ages of 13 and 17 alleged to have participated in the incident have been identified, police said, and arrests are expected after the pending investigation. A father of one of the youths was quoted as saying, "After the kicking and carrying on my son didn't do anything more than anyone else." Police gave this account: Bowers and three friends had ridden their bikes to a small park area at the end of the county bike trail where a railroad overpass can be seen from Roosevelt Road. A late-model station wagon occupied by three youths stopped and exchanged "obscenities and epithets" with the bicyclists. One youth allegedly said, "I'll be back" and returned with six more youths and a fight began. Two youths with Bowers received minor lacerations. A neighbor reported that Bower's girlfriend, who was at the scene when the fight began, grabbed the victim's 19-speed bike and went for help.*

* A few of the wordings in this passage can be found in poorly-sourced material somewhere on the internet.

Acknowledgements

Thanks to David Ossman, who always came into the Mark Time Radio Shows reading the prose poems so effortlessly they sounded like they were just made up on the spot. Thanks to a crowd of other wonderful actors, including Dion Graham, Jane Oppenheimer, Eleanor Price, and Rich Fish.

Thanks to the many musicians I've had the pleasure to work with, including Rev. Dwight Frizzell, Pat Conway, Julia Thro, Mike Wheaton, Eleanor Price, and Jason Kao Hwang.

Thanks to my two oldest, most trusted collaborators: Mike Wheaton for all the songwriting we've done over the years, and many thanks and laughs to my Great Northern Audio Theatre partner, Jerry Stearns. Thanks to Marjorie Van Halteren for becoming a character as well as a collaborator in our work on her *That Tuesday* podcast.

Thanks to the many artists at the National Audio Theatre Festivals and to the CONvergence Science Fiction conventions for allowing us to perform for them.

Thanks to designer and copy editor, Evie Brosius. Thanks to my wife, Arla Bush. And a special thanks to my daughter, Eleanor Price, for her project management and editorial expertise. This shiny book was a long time coming and would not have been possible without their patient and understanding help.

And, of course, thank you all for reading and listening.

BRIAN PRICE,

AN AUDIO THEATER PRODUCER, WRITER, AND DIRECTOR, has been working in radio and audio publishing since the early 1980s. He first sold 90-second comedic monologues to *The Daily Feed* in Washington, D.C., and later that decade became a producer and director for the Midwest Radio Theatre Workshop. He was a frequent contributor to the *Iowa Radio Project* in the early 1990s, and was producer/director for the *Dakota Reader,* the Grist Mill horror series, and the Native Voices at the Autry in the 2000s. His short skits, plays, and monologues have been performed by community troupes across the country and two of his plays have been translated into Croatian and Chinese. In 1994 he formed the Great Northern Audio Theatre company with frequent collaborator, Jerry Stearns. Although they've often been paid in T-shirts and "gimme hats" for their original productions, their partnership has led to Brian and Jerry receiving the Mark Time Grand Master Award for Lifetime Achievement in Science Fiction Audio in 2013, the Norman Corwin Award for Excellence in Audio Theatre in 2017, and an APA Audie Award for Best in Audio Drama in 2017 for *In The Embers*. Brian was also nominated for a 2019 Audie for *The Old Cart Wrangler's Saga*. Much of his recorded work including his audiobook novel, *The Recollections of Turner Ashbey,* can be found at: www.downpour.com/catalogsearch/result/?q=Brian+Price

Although he and his family have lived all over the Midwest from Missouri to Iowa to South Dakota to Indiana, he was born and grew up in Arlington, Virginia, and still misses the Appalachian Mountains.